BERRIES ON THE HEATHER

BERRIES ON THE HEATHER

KARI WILLIAMSON

The Shetland Times Ltd.
Lerwick
2007

Berries On The Heather

ISBN 978-1-904746-30-0

Cover designed by Kari Williamson.

First published by The Shetland Times Ltd., 2007

A catalogue record for this book is available from the British Library.

This novel is entirely a work of fiction. The names, characters and incidents
portrayed in it are the work of the author's imagination. Any resemblance to
actual persons, living or dead, events or localities is entirely coincidental.

Printed and published by
The Shetland Times Ltd., Gremista, Lerwick,
Shetland ZE1 0PX, Scotland.

Dedicated to my parents, Tamar and Willie,
who always encouraged me to write

CONTENTS

Chapter 1

GRINDA GARTH

IT WAS one of those evenings when it was good to be indoors in the glow of the peat-fire; an evening in that No-Man's-Land in time when Christmas is over and New Year still to come.

All day, showers of wet snow had swept across the dun-coloured landscape like smoky banners, but the showers had turned to hail with the darkening and it had begun to freeze. The real winter was just setting in. The village of Aestervoe, straggling along the hillside, turned its back to the north-east, each grey stone house a little sanctuary of snugness and warmth.

The old croft house of Grinda Garth, standing furthest up the hill, looked down on its neighbours and huddled its long, low structure amongst its out-buildings, the barn and byre at one side, the lambhouse at the back. Along the northern perimeter of the garden a row of ancient and unlovely bore trees poked stunted and twisted branches towards the hills above; bleak hills, in wintertime, and scarred by centuries of peat-cutting. But in the south corner, a willow waved slender grey fingers against the sky, and further along two thriving sycamores stood sturdy and firm, scarcely moved by the bitter wind. The flower-beds were covered by the mouldy residue of leaves, but within a few weeks the daffodils would begin to thrust pointed green noses up through the earth and the dead vegetation would help protect the shoots from the frost.

In the big living-room of Grinda Garth, the peat-fire blazed on the open hearth and cast rosy shadows on the whitened sides of the chimney. The paper garlands, which hung from corner to corner across the white-distempered beams of the ceiling, swayed and rustled softly in the rising warm air. Dangling from the hook-and-chain above the flames, the black kettle began to sing.

Kirsty Mouat put down her knitting and got up to make the eight o'clock's tea; a short, roly-poly woman wearing a black wool dress and dark grey cardigan; the dress protected by a black pinarette sprigged with tiny purple flowers of some obscure species, stiff and shiny with first-time-on newness. Her dark hair scarcely touched with grey in spite of her sixty-odd years was worn in a style of former days, with a neat centre parting and plaits rolled round against her ears.

She crossed to the hearth to pick up the teapot and, on the rag-rug, Tammas, the cat, eyed her plaid slippers with suspicion and drew himself a little farther away.

In one of the out-bye corners of the room her husband, Magnie, was cutting turnips for the lambs of the previous summer, the pieces falling into the zinc bucket with a musical clang which diminished as the bucket became full. A quiet man, with a shock of wiry, silvery hair, his movements were slow and deliberate. Their eldest son Davie, a widower, who had returned to his parents' home on the death of his wife, was half-asleep behind a copy of the local newspaper after a day spent driving a truck 'on the roads'.

On the long, wooden settle, known as the 'restin-shair', Davie's three young daughters pretended to read, but in reality were listening to the conversation of the adults. The conversation was more loquacious than usual tonight for there was a visitor, Auntie Charlotte, Kirsty's married sister from the house across the burn, Leabakka.

Auntie Charlotte had a fine flow of words, and while she talked the short, thick aluminium needles flew in and out of the spencer she was knitting so quickly it was impossible to follow their movements. She had been made to sit in the 'best' chair which stood at one side of the hearth and had a button-back and was covered in brown American cloth.

"You'll come over to us on New Year's Day," she was saying. "You haven't heard the wireless Johnny sent home to us for Christmas, and Gracie Fields is going to be on."

"My, I would like to hear that," said Kirsty, as she set out cups and plates on the table. "We've got some of her records, but it would be fine to hear her in the flesh, so to speak."

"It's a splendid wireless!" Charlotte said, proudly. "That clear – you never miss a word. And the programmes – the weather forecast, and the Children's Hour! Well, I don't know how we managed without it."

Kirsty was busy buttering slices of currant tea-loaf while, from underneath the restin-shair, Gaerd, the sheepdog, sprawled amongst the family's boots and shoes, regarded her hopefully with deceptively sad brown eyes. Perhaps if he looked pathetic enough she would cut off a crust and throw it to him.

"Johnny didn't manage home for Christmas," Kirsty remarked.

"He decided to go another trip with the ship, to Vancouver this time, and come home later on – about March, maybe – if he's spared."

"March? Will he stay home for long, do you know, Auntie Charlotte? Through the summer, perhaps?" It was the girl who sat opposite her across the hearth, who spoke.

Charlotte glanced at her shrewdly. "I couldn't say, for sure, but likely he will. We'll be having your wedding when the summer comes, Joey," she added.

Joey bent her head further over her knitting, so that her soft brown hair fell forward and obscured her face, hiding the pink which tinged her cheeks. The single diamond of her ring glinted as she made a pretence of counting the stitches on her needle. "Well, perhaps. All going well."

"I'll need to get a new frock for that event!" Charlotte continued. "Nina wanted me to buy one for Christmas. Said I couldn't wear my brown cashmere for another year. But I never bothered, for where would I be going to wear it, even at a Christmas time?"

On the restin-shair, Marina, the youngest of the three little girls, wriggled, curling her legs in their fawn woollen stockings underneath her, and remarking, "You went to the Tree in the hall, Auntie Charlotte." She lisped slightly for, at six years old, she had lost her front baby teeth.

Charlotte looked up, as if aware of the presence of the children for the first time.

"That's true," she sounded mildly surprised. "But, then, I never had my coat off. It's as cold as an ice-house, that hall."

Caroline, who was eight, scowled at Marina and nudged her sharply. Why did Marina have to butt in, just when the conversation had turned to Joey's wedding? She had wanted to find out all she could about that and, by experience, she had discovered that the one sure way of hearing things was by not drawing attention to oneself.

Marina said, absently, "Stop it, Caro," and addressed herself again to her great-aunt. "But wasn't it lovely when they put out all the lamps and lit the candles and the Chinese lanterns?"

"Oh, fine," agreed Charlotte, with a marked lack of enthusiasm. "But I'm always feared it'll all catch fire. A blazing inferno, it would be, and not one of us left to tell the tale."

Marina fell silent, contemplating this unimagined termination to the Christmas party.

"Ah well, we must all trust in Providence," said Kirsty.

With Joey's help she began to pass round the tea, going first to Charlotte for she was the guest. Charlotte took the tin tray with the picture of the *Cutty Sark* on it and placed it on her almost non-existent lap.

Davie took his cup in a work-worn hand and, as a particularly heavy blast of wind struck the window, said, "If this wind keeps up I'm doubtful if the steamer will come tomorrow."

"We'll soon have the new steamer. They say it's to be ready in August," said Charlotte. "You'll need to steer clear of that date for your wedding, Joey, for we'll need to turn out to a man to cheer its arrival."

Joey smiled. "I'll remember that."

The repast over, the two men got ready to do the night work, putting on Wellingtons and tying 'luggit' caps securely. Davie lit the Tilley lantern and took down the milking-pail from its hook in the porch. Magnie would put by the lambs and then shut Gaerd in the barn for the night, with a supper of potatoes and skimmed milk.

Kirsty poured the remainder of the water from the black kettle into the washing-up basin, then glanced towards the three children. "Now, bairns, you'll have to be getting off to bed."

"I'll need to wash my feet tonight," Caro said, glibly, knowing that the kettle would have to be re-filled and boiled again before this could be accomplished. With luck, she'd be able to drag out the time for another half-hour.

But Joey put an end to her hopes. "You did that last night, Caro, and so did Marina and Connie, and you've just been around the house all day, never over the doorstep. Your feet are perfectly all right, so away you go."

"You'll have to go up with them, Joey, for last night they were sky-larking around an hour or more after they went up. The minister and his wife came in and I couldn't very well leave them sitting and go to see what was going on. Twice over I had to go between the doors and knock up with the tongs. I was black-affrontit."

"It wasn't me. I was in bed. I couldn't get peace to sleep for the noise Caro and Marina made," Connie said, virtuously.

"Hhm! I've seen the day when you weren't far behind in any mischief that was going," Kirsty replied.

Joey shepherded the reluctant youngsters up the stairs while Charlotte picked up her knitting again and she and Kirsty began to chat in a desultory fashion about the weather. But Charlotte's mind, at least, seemed to be elsewhere. During a lull in the conversation, she said, "You'll fairly miss Joey when she goes."

Kirsty picked up a crust and tossed it to Tammas, who sniffed at it disdainfully.

"Young folk have their own lives to live."

"Well, maybe she's made a good match." Charlotte's needles clicked in and out of the stitches more furiously than ever. "After all, Hugh Sutherland has been going to sea since a boy and nothing and nobody to spend a halfpenny on. He must have a few pennies put by him now. And he's not a youth – how old will he be? Thirty-six? Mind, I think he's a bit old for Joey, set in his ways, no doubt. Is fourteen years not too much? What think you, Kirsty?"

"Joey will just have to please herself," Kirsty replied, but there was something in her tone which implied that she was not wholly in disagreement with her sister.

Charlotte paused in her efforts, the knitting slipping to her lap, her hands still. "He was to have been married once before, I mind, to a minister's daughter from Sandside. Then she threw him over – or maybe it was the other way round. It must be close on ten years ago and I never did hear all the ins and outs of it."

Kirsty was silent for a moment or two, then she spoke hesitantly, as if unsure whether to voice her thoughts or not. "There was talk of another girl once – someone in the south …"

"That's true," Charlotte nodded. "That fell through, as well. Oh well, he seems all set now, and he couldn't have made a better choice than Joey. She'll make a good wife."

"Yes, she's young, but she's capable, and used to hard work." But there was still anxiety in Kirsty's eyes, and in the tone of her voice.

Charlotte's glance was calculating. "Oh, those days will soon be over for Joey! They're renting the old Hivdalea place, I hear? And not going to work the croft?"

"They're planning to fix it up. The roof's in poor condition and it needs a new porch for the old one was blown down by that bad gale we had last October."

"I hear there's talk of heightening the house so as to do away with the coom-ceilings upstairs, and of converting one of the small bedrooms into a bathroom, no less ..."

There was no mistaking Kirsty's sniff. She put the dishes back into the cupboard with a rattle. "Hhm! A right show place it's to be, according to him. But there's no start been made yet and he rejoins his ship next month. They'll be married in summer and moving in, and if it isn't done before I can't see it being done afterwards. I have no doubt Joey will have to be like the rest of us, have to sole her socks with less cloth. Not that she'll mind, poor lass, for she's not been used to so much."

Charlotte picked up her knitting again. "Maybe he'll employ someone to do the work. He should be well able to afford it!"

Kirsty sniffed again. "I'd rather see it than hear of it."

"Well, as long as he makes her a good, kind man, that's all that matters."

The cynicism and vexation seemed to drain away from Kirsty's face, but she still looked ill-at-ease, and worried. "In my opinion, my Charlotte, Joey has thrown her cap over the windmill. But I'll not be the one to tell her so!"

Upstairs, the three small girls had settled down in bed without further protest. Joey turned down the wick of the lamp and blew out the remaining meagre flame, then said good night. Crossing the narrow landing to the bedroom occupied by Kirsty and Magnie, she laid a couple of peats on the smouldering embers of the fire "to keep a warm air," as Kirsty put it.

She drew back the curtains and looked out into the bleak night. Across the voe, the lights of the houses were pinpricks in the darkness. On Gardie Hill shone the solitary light of the house where the Sutherlands lived: Hugh, his parents, and two older sisters. Joey had failed to make any friendly contact with May and Belle. Their attitude towards her was a sort of casual aloofness, a barrier she could never get beyond. She felt that she knew them no better now than in the days before she had become engaged to Hugh.

She sighed, remembering that May, the elder of the two, was to be her bridesmaid. It did seem rather ridiculous to have a bridesmaid of forty when the bride was only twenty-two. Sometimes it gave her an uncomfortable jolt to realise that Hugh, himself, was thirty-six.

She let the curtain drop into place and turned away, thinking about the dresses that would have to be ordered soon. With May's lank, greying hair, her sallow complexion, and sharp features, it would not be easy to find anything to flatter her.

Later, when Charlotte had departed for home, escorted by Davie with the lantern, Kirsty laid aside her knitting for the night and relaxed for a moment before setting the supper. In the porch, Magnie could be heard rummaging through the bunker in search of resting-peats which would preserve kindling throughout the night.

Joey began to do a little perfunctory tidying-up, removing Caro's long woollen stockings from the back of the chair where she had tossed them following her declaration that her feet had to be washed. In the morning, she would indignantly demand to know what had become of them, blaming everyone but herself for their disappearance. On the linoleum, in front of the restin-shair, Marina's hair-ribbon lay like a crumpled blue flower.

Connie, the eldest, who was plump, placid, and tidy, had left none of her belongings behind.

"I've promised Charlotte we'll go over on New Year's Day, after dinner," said Kirsty. "You'll be going to the social at Wastervoe, likely?"

"Yes. I'll take my dance-frock over to Leabakka and get dressed there."

"Davie said something about taking the bairns, if it's a fine night. We won't mention it to them until we see, though."

"Hugh is borrowing a car from someone. He'll be able to take all of us, the girls aren't so big."

"That'll be fine." Kirsty got up and began to see to the supper, pouring milk into the pan to heat.

With sudden misgiving, Joey wondered how Hugh would react to being saddled with the three children, and Davie.

Chapter 2

NEW YEAR'S EVE

JOEY Reid scarcely remembered that Kirsty and Magnie were not her parents; that her father had been lost at sea when she was six months old, and had been Kirsty's brother. She had been ten when her mother had died from consumption and Kirsty had 'taken her in'. Neither by word nor action had she been made to feel an outsider in the Mouat household.

Davie had been a young man, and delighted, in his quiet way, by the addition of a small girl to the family. Each weekend, there had been sweets or an inexpensive toy for her, bought out of his hard-earned and meagre wages. Arthur, the Mouats' younger son, had been Joey's senior by three years and, not unnaturally, there had been a few squalls and disagreements between the two, for Arthur had been at an age when it was obligatory to despise all girls; also he had been aggravated by what he considered an intrusion into his private life whenever Joey had attempted to join him and his male companions in their pastimes.

Kirsty had always taken the girl's part, remonstrating with her son, pointing out that, being the elder, he ought to be more forbearing, and Arthur had, to his credit, accepted this; glumly, but without lasting resentment.

Joey's relationship with Willa Bairnson had been rather different. Willa was the daughter of Kirsty and Charlotte's eldest sister, long since dead, and she had always considered herself to stand in lieu of a daughter to Kirsty and Magnie. Although she had been twenty-six and married for a year to Tom Bain when Joey had come to Grinda Garth, she resented Kirsty's obvious affection for the child; and although she could not have expressed it in words, she had the feeling that Kirsty and Joey were the same kind of people – kindred spirits, as it were – in a way that she had never been.

Willa was of a sour disposition, maintaining that all children should be subjected to the strictest discipline. "Children are young animals, they have to be brought to heel," was her oft-repeated maxim, but one that she had no chance to put into practise as she and Tom had no family. Her only training attempts had been inflicted on Joey, a reserved child who had little need of them. Willa had not endeared herself to Joey. Fortunately, she had her own domain, Hjarkland, just down the road from Grinda Garth, on the village road.

On the morning of New Year's Eve Joey, glancing out of the window, saw Willa trudging up the Grinda Garth road. "Here's Willa," she remarked, her tone expressing little cordiality.

Kirsty was preparing the hens' morning feed, mashing potatoes in an old enamel basin, using a bottle. "She's early on the go," she replied, and measured out a spoonful of red, pungent-smelling Karswood Spice to sprinkle into the mash. "Maybe she's needing the milk early."

"I don't think so. She hasn't got the pail."

Willa came in, breathing hard, her face crimson from the exertion of walking uphill against the biting wind. Like her two aunts, she was short and stout, but lacked their unexpected agility. She slumped down now onto the nearest chair and began to unbutton her coat.

"I just ran up," she said, inaccurately. "It's dreary when you're on your own. Tom had to work today. As I said, they might have given him the day off, it being New Year, but there was no word of that!" She seemed to imply that it was Tom's fault entirely.

She looked round the room, taking in Joey washing up the breakfast dishes; the children playing on the restin-shair with 'paper folk', figures cut from fashion catalogues; and Kirsty, in the act of putting her brown shawl over her head and crossing it over to tie behind her at the waist. The discontented droop of Willa's lips became more pronounced.

"You oughtn't to be going out on a day like this," she said to Kirsty. "That's for young folk."

"It's a fine enough day, for a winter's day, and I'll do what I can while I'm able," Kirsty retorted, with some asperity. "I'm not tottering on the brink just yet!"

Joey, having no desire to be left alone to listen to the moans of Willa, said hurriedly, "I'll see to the hens as soon as I've finished the dishes."

"If you would, Joey. I'll have to start the milking. We're late getting underway this morning." Kirsty set her slippers neatly on the hearthstone and began to pull on an old pair of men's socks over her own black cashmere stockings. "Magnie's gone to look at the fence of the north-by park, for the ram got out yesterday and the Mansons thought he was going to get amongst their cross-ewes and there was a fine how-d'you-do before he was rounded up." She hauled on her rubber-boots which had been warming, soles to the fire.

"I could milk Flekka," Joey began, "But Bonnie ..."

"Oh, Bonnie won't stand for you. She's got the very Old Fellow in her, that cow."

Willa threw her coat untidily across the arm of the restin-shair, scattering 'paper folk' in all directions. Connie began to retrieve them, while Caro and Marina scowled at Willa's broad back, but knew better than to say anything. Willa produced a piece of knitting and settled herself in the armchair beside the fire. She didn't offer to help with any of the household chores.

Kirsty diagnosed Willa's peevish discontent as stemming from "having too little to do," but Joey, privately, disagreed. Willa only did a minimum of housework in her own home, and she didn't even try to manage on Tom's wages which ought to have been adequate for the two of them. She was always borrowing from Kirsty, and from Charlotte – tea, sugar, flour – and she was kept supplied with both milk and eggs from Grinda Garth. There was, Joey considered, plenty with which Willa might have kept herself occupied, had she wanted to.

At the back of one o'clock, Tom Bain arrived. "Got the rest of the day off. Managed to persuade the foreman. Don't think he was too keen on working any longer himself." Tom laughed.

Tom was always laughing. It was difficult to decide if Tom was a saint or a simpleton. He had to be one or the other, to make a habit of laughter while married to Willa.

Perversely Willa, who had grumbled because Tom had gone to work in the morning, now seemed put out by his unexpected return, and she accompanied him home with no good grace.

Soon after they left, Arthur arrived home. A tall, slim young man, with his mother's dark hair and his Auntie Charlotte's brown eyes, Arthur worked at the store attached to the village shop, dealing with such items as tar, paraffin, bran, and sheep-dip. He also made one of the crew of the sixern, the boat which brought ashore the goods from the inter-island steamer which called thrice weekly.

After he had had his dinner, he set to with great vigour to construct his guizing outfit for later that night. The custom of guizing – dressing in fancy-dress and visiting every house in the village on New Year's Eve – dated so far back that its origin had long been forgotten, but it was still adhered to by the young people, and eagerly anticipated by the old who stayed at home.

In no time at all, the living-room was in a state of wild disorder. Joey, returning from shutting the hens in for the night, paused to take stock of it. Fragments of some black material littered the floor and the restin-shair. She recognised it as an old coat which Kirsty had worn on cold days for work around the croft until it had become too tattered even for that. Strands of wool seemed to be everywhere.

"This room is like a battle-field!" she exclaimed, half-laughing, half-aghast. "What on earth are you making?"

Arthur raised a flushed and ill-humoured countenance. "It's a Mickey Mouse costume. It's more difficult to make than I thought it would be."

"What are these lengths of wool for?"

"Whiskers. Only it doesn't work. Too limp." He picked off a few strands which were clinging to his jumper and dropped them into the peat-basket.

"You'll have to get a move on. We're supposed to muster at five o'clock," Joey pointed out.

"In my young day, we had our outfits ready weeks ahead, but it's leave everything to the last minute nowadays," said Kirsty.

"Maybe you didn't have as much work to do as I have," Arthur said, irritably.

"Work! My bairn, you don't know what work is. I could tell you ..." but she broke off to say, "ease the lid off the pot, would you, Joey?"

Kirsty was working at the table, making sheep's-puddings, mixing oatmeal, a little flour, onions and fat together in a large bowl. The black pot was boiling over the fire, the steam adding to the discomfort of the room.

Joey obeyed, saying to Arthur in passing, "I don't think I can spare the time to give you a hand ..."

"Oh, he'll maybe finish that in time for next New Year," Kirsty said, with heavy humour. She began to fill a long, narrow skin with the mixture, pushing it in and shaking it down.

"I shall have it ready for tonight!" Arthur declared. He picked up part of his costume, a tapering length clumsily stitched together to represent a tail, and began to stuff it with scraps of wool. The similarity between Arthur stuffing the tail and Kirsty filling the pudding-skin was too much for Joey. She collapsed on a chair, overcome with helpless laughter, while both Arthur and Kirsty paused in their endeavours to gape at her.

"You should be helping with the puddings, Arthur. You'd be a dab hand at it!" she gasped.

Kirsty's features relaxed in a grim smile. "He'd have looked down his nose if I'd asked him."

Arthur gave them both a contemptuous look and carried on with his task.

He and Joey had an early tea, and then Joey went upstairs to dress, reappearing shortly in a suit of plus-fours, bought from a jumble sale the previous autumn with the guizing in mind. The little girls crowded round her in high glee. Arthur had been forced, reluctantly, to abandon his Mickey Mouse costume through lack of time, and he finally appeared draped in a cast-off sheet and with a patterned scarf for a cummerbund, and looking morose.

Marina hopped round him. "What are you supposed to be, Uncle Arthur? A ghost?"

"A sheik," Arthur responded, a little self-consciously. "Do I look OK, Mam? Joey?"

"Oh, dashing," Joey answered.

"I like something comical myself," said Kirsty, "but you'll do."

Arthur continued to look unconvinced.

"Here are your false-faces." Caro grovelled amongst the remains of black material which still littered the restin-shair and produced two masks.

"I'm going to look stupid, a Mickey Mouse mask with this outfit," Arthur said, unhappily.

"Och, it's only for fun, you're not trying to win a prize," his mother adjured him.

As the door closed behind Joey and Arthur, Kirsty sighed with relief. "I'll surely get the house redd-up now. The guizers won't be here before the back of nine."

"And can we sit up after that, to see the New Year in? And the first footers?" asked Caro.

"My bairn, you'll be dropping over with sleep long before that time comes. And it's not likely we'll have any first footers this night. We're too far off the beaten track away up here. You'd better go early to your beds and be fresh for going over to your Auntie Charlotte's tomorrow."

By the time the guizing was over, and Joey and Arthur had returned home to change into less exotic attire before going out first-footing, Hugh Sutherland had arrived.

Kirsty, who was rarely at a loss for words, never felt altogether comfortable with Hugh. She invariably found herself having to rack her mind for something to say and her resultant remarks sounded both pointless and foolish to her own ears, the maudlin ponderings of an old woman. In all honesty, she felt she couldn't blame him for the faintly patronising manner he adopted towards her.

Neither Magnie nor Davie were at all over-awed by Hugh but, as neither were talkative, the conversation languished. Though Hugh always found plenty to say. He was a tall man, fairish, good-looking in a bland sort of way, but already he was developing signs of heaviness round the waist, and in the set of his shoulders. "Stuffed shirt," Arthur called him, but never in Joey's hearing.

After midnight, the young people departed on their various expeditions, even Davie, who set off to visit Willa and Tom and a few neighbouring houses. Arthur looked more cheerful now as he left, dressed in his second-best suit. The cause of his eagerness to wear the ill-fated Mickey Mouse costume had been revealed when the red-haired school-teacher had appeared as an attractive Minnie Mouse, the shortness of whose skirt above the black silk stockings had made Kirsty's mouth purse in silent disapproval. There had been several Mickey Mice amongst the male guizers, in costumes made with varying degrees of incompetence …

The children had gone to bed long since. Kirsty and Magnie settled by the fire for the first real rest, and peace, that day. Magnie got his pipe going and reached for his magazine, *Sea Breezes*. Kirsty, for once, let her hands lie idly in her lap. She gazed at the leaping flames and upbraided herself mentally for allowing sentiment to run away with her as always happened each New Year. It was impossible for her thoughts not to turn to former years, and to people who only lived in memory, now.

Her parents; her hard-working, placid mother, and her father, an imposing figure with a thick, dark beard, kindly at heart, yet a little awe-inspiring to his children. She recalled how, as a small girl, she had run barefoot to the beach to watch the fishing boats with their huge, red sails, come in. They had been hard times; although life still wasn't easy at least there was a measure of security. No longer could a landlord demand a share of a boat's catch, nor could he turn his tenants out of their crofts on a whim.

Her thoughts turned to her brother John, and Phemie his wife, and the day their only child had been christened in the little church at Wastervoe. She recalled the dark oak pews and the stained-glass window behind the choir-stalls where the afternoon sun had streamed through and touched the white hair of the old minister with jig-saw pieces of red and blue.

"Joey Euphemia …" She could hear his voice still in the drowsy hush of the summer's day.

And in the churchyard across the burn, Davie's wife had been buried on a bitter day in March, four years ago. Poor Lily! But she and Davie had been happy in the eight years they had had together.

Lily had been a great one for reading, and with a special interest in the doings of the Royal family, which was how her youngest daughter bore the name of Marina, after the young Greek princess whose name had been linked with that of Prince George. They were married now – the Duke and Duchess of Kent – but Lily had not lived to hear of that event which had excited the whole country in November 1934, eight months after she had died.

Without realising it, Kirsty's thoughts wandered into the present. How, she wondered, would Davie's future continue? She would like to see him married again, to someone cheerful and capable, and not at all like poor Lily who had been rather a dreamer. But maybe he wouldn't want that. Perhaps, in their own hearts, everyone knew what was best for themselves and it wouldn't be as other folk thought.

Joey, for instance, maybe she knew … But Kirsty shook her head. She had a feeling that Joey would grow away from the family once she was married to Hugh Sutherland. He would see to that, even though this rarely happened in the close-knit island community. She felt that that would not happen if Joey married some other young man of her acquaintance. There was something about Hugh, as if he despised the stock from which he had come.

Kirsty smiled to herself. Now she was being fanciful! What would Charlotte, always so practical, have to say if she knew her thoughts? But, then, Charlotte could afford to be practical. She seemed to have few worries where her family was concerned. In the summer, Johnny would be coming home and his presence was enough to cheer anyone. "A proper caution," Kirsty dubbed him, as one who was full of fun and good-humour. And Nina, his sister, was a plain, but pleasant girl, popular with everyone and fancy-free.

Oh well, Joey would go her own road, but life would go on, and the three small girls upstairs would still need her, Kirsty thought, with a sudden uplifting of spirits. It was strange how things worked out. Just when her own family were beginning to fend for themselves, Joey had come to them, needing their care. And after that there had been Davie's motherless lasses. At a time of life when most folk were being left behind, she and Magnie were never more in the thick of things, surrounded by young people who depended on them. They were lucky, and those folk who said, "It's too much for you, at your age," didn't know what they were talking about!

Kirsty got to her feet and Tammas, the cat, woke with a start and glared at her out of cold, green, oval eyes, then yawned, and stretched out a paw.

"I'll just get each of us a cup of milk, Magnie, then we'll make for bed," she said. "We'll leave the wall-back screwed down low, in the porch, for the young ones coming in."

Magnie, pre-occupied with the saga of the tea-clippers, his reading-glasses slipping down his nose, grunted, his usual reply.

Chapter Three

A NIGHT OUT

"I'VE been dying to show you this!" Nina produced Oxendale's winter catalogue and began to flick over the pages.

Joey had unpacked her dress from the ancient fibre case and was spreading it out on the chest which stood below the skylight in Nina's bedroom. She came to peer over her cousin's shoulder.

From downstairs, there filtered the sound of the new wireless, where the older folk and the little girls were listening to Harry Lauder. They had all come over from Grinda Garth in the afternoon, except for Davie who had remained to see to the night-work, and Arthur who, as Kirsty said, "Had other fish to fry!"

The day had been frosty, cold and dry, with little wind. In a clear, greenish sky, the new moon had come up, a silver sliver. The children were going to be lucky and be allowed to go to the concert at Wastervoe.

"Look!" Nina paused at a page of dance-dresses and pointed to a spectacular creation with one half of its skirt black, the other red. On the bodice, the colours were reversed. "That's the frock I'm having for your wedding!"

"It's gorgeous! I couldn't wear it, too showy, but it'll suit you, Nina." There was a tiny tinge of envy in Joey's voice.

Nina was not conventionally pretty. Her mousy brown hair and grey eyes were nondescript, but she had a vivacity and sparkle which made her seem attractive; it also made her popular. Joey, on the other hand, although she had a soft prettiness, was on the quiet side. She had always been reserved, and a little diffident, even as a child.

Joey looked closer at the sketch of the dress. "Nina! It costs thirty-eight shillings!"

Nina giggled. "Yes! Isn't it awful of me? Don't let Mammy know! I've been saving my egg-money for absolute ages, and Dad is going to help me out. He got a good price for the ox that was sold at the October roup. After all," she added, "you'll only be getting married the once."

"I suppose so," Joey smiled. "I haven't ordered my own dress yet. Hugh wants me to go to Lerwick and have it made at Gifford and Brown's, but ..." She left the sentence unfinished and Nina gave her an understanding glance.

"That's the made-to-measure place. It'll be terribly expensive there, won't it?"

Joey looked troubled. "I imagine so. May and Belle are going there."

"Yes, well, I daresay they can afford it. Their father was a merchant until he retired, well-feathered, by all accounts." Nina stopped, flushing a little as she remembered, too late, that she was speaking of Joey's future in-laws.

Joey didn't seem to mind. "I ought to have tried for work at the herring-station last summer."

"I'd hate to work on the herring-station! You would, too. Gutting fish – ugh!"

"A lot of the girls seem to like it," Joey said, doubtfully. "They're always on about the fun they have."

"Oh, the fun would be fine. It's the work I shouldn't care for. Besides," Nina added, with a shrewdness inherited from her mother and her aunt, "I'm sure Hugh wouldn't want his intended working on a fishing-station ..."

Joey sighed, but made no reply, and presently, she asked, "How are you getting to Wastervoe tonight? It's a pity the car isn't large enough to take us all."

Nina slipped her dress of blue, crepe-backed marocain over her head and began to do up the buttons. "Oh, walking with the Hoseason girls, and Ruby and Ina, and probably Cissie and Jean, as well. I wish you were coming with us, Joey."

For a moment, Joey wished the same. She had missed the companionship of the old crowd; walking to the dances at Wastervoe, and to church or chapel meetings on summer evenings. The silly, carefree chatter, and the laughter which exploded out of nothing. She silently reproved herself. Everyone, she supposed, had vague regrets at leaving their heedless youth behind!

But it wouldn't last, once she was settled down in her own home with Hugh. She fastened a single strand of Ciro pearls (Hugh's Christmas present) round her neck, and twitched up the shoulders of her sea-green taffeta dress.

Nina was pinning the hem of her long skirt up round her waist. "I'm sure it will be a crumpled mess by the time I reach the hall, but I can't walk all that way with it flapping round my legs and getting splashed with mud and mortar. And I'll have to wear rubber boots!" she added, disgustedly, with a glance at the neat silver sandals standing under the dressing-table waiting to be popped into the slipper-bag. "Talk about spoiling the effect!"

Downstairs, Harry Lauder had just finished singing *Keep Right on to the End of the Road*, and now the announcer was giving out details of the jazz programme that was to follow.

"Tch, tch!" Charlotte shook her head, not thinking much of that. She stood on tiptoe to reach the shelf and switched off the wireless with a snap. It had been fine while it lasted but now she and Kirsty would have a chance to converse.

Gibbie, her husband, and Magnie, had already begun to talk together. Gibbie was a thin, spry, little man, with a white moustache and sparse white hair. He talked; of his sea-faring days, of men they had both known, of humorous incidents, and of how people had reacted in various situations. Magnie sat with a half-smile on his lips, his pipe in his hand, nodding or shaking his head, never contributing more than half-a-dozen words at a time, but obviously enjoying himself.

But it wouldn't be long before Gibbie returned to the subject of the news in the papers. Charlotte was disapproving when he would read out items aloud, shake his head, and mutter darkly about "another war."

"Wheest with you, boy," she would say, and would refuse to enter into any discussion about it. She didn't want to think about such things. Neither did anyone else ... but there was something terrifyingly convincing in Gibbie's observations.

The children, who had been playing at the table with Nina's old doll's house, had grown a little restless as the time approached for them to leave for the concert. Marina and Caro played in a desultory fashion with the kitten; Connie glanced through the pile of papers and magazines which lay on a stool in the corner but there was nothing amongst them which caught her interest. Mostly, they were Uncle Gibbie's newspapers, except for the *Christian Herald* and the *People's Friend*.

She whiled away the time by reading 'Will and Wag' on the children's page of the *People's Friend*, and then reading the captions under the pictures illustrating the stories.

Nina came downstairs and the girls stared at her with admiration. How good it must be to be grown-up, wear a long dress, and be going to a dance! There was nothing more to be desired.

Nina went off amid admonishments from her mother not to stay out "till all hours," to remember to wear her scarf coming home, and warnings as to what would happen because she hadn't put on her wool camisole underneath her dance-frock when it had been prepared for her. It was, Charlotte said, still lying ironed on the ben table.

At long last, as it seemed, the girls were told to get their coats on; they were their best winter coats with matching hats. Then, with Joey, they set off for the road. There was no proper path between Leabakka and the road, only a track made by the passage of feet through the marshy grass.

Davie was just coming up the road as they reached it, wearing his good, navy serge suit, a little shiny now when seen in the stark light of day, but it would be dim in the hall. Not that it would worry Davie.

Hugh was late. They had been waiting for a full fifteen minutes before the lights of the car appeared. Joey, despite her heavy coat, was conscious of the cold taffeta clinging to her arms and back, while the children were almost weeping with disappointment, sure that something had happened to prevent them from ever getting to the concert. Apart from their anticipation of the unexpected treat, Connie and Caro had another reason for wishing to go to Wastervoe. For weeks beforehand, the 'big girls' at the Aestervoe school had been boasting that they were to attend the dance following the concert, and had systematically tormented the 'kids', as they called them, by their grown-up airs, and much discussion of new frocks for the occasion. Marina, who was still in the infants' class, wasn't much interested, but Connie and Caro were agog to see fat Winnie Herculeson in floral crepe-de-chine, not to mention pimply Annie Irvine in tangerine georgette.

Hugh was more than a little irritable when he arrived. Apparently, when he had gone to pick up the car the owner had been in the act of mending a puncture and this had caused the delay. Now, he urged them into the car impatiently as if they were the ones who were late. Davie, true to form, said very little. Joey felt displeased by Hugh's attitude but, knowing that he hadn't been too enthusiastic about taking Davie and the children with them in the first place, she tried not to irritate him still further.

The hall was filling up by the time they reached it. Through the windows, they could see the organisers agitatedly setting extra seats.

"Do you really want to go in?" Hugh asked Joey. "Wouldn't you rather come up to the house and see the old folks, wait until the dance starts? This concert – it'll be the usual drivel."

Joey felt that she had been placed in an awkward situation. It would seem ungracious to turn down Hugh's invitation, for his parents were old and would be alone, as both May and Belle would certainly be attending the evening's entertainment.

She looked down at the faces of the three small girls, illuminated by the light streaming through the open door of the hall. This was a big event in their young lives and she wanted to be there to share it, to watch their reactions and enjoy their enjoyment. Nothing else would be spoken about for weeks to come – rather a grim thought! But she knew that Hugh would understand none of this.

Hesitantly, she said, "I don't know, Hugh – the girls – I think I must stay with them …"

"They've got their father!" Hugh pointed out. But then his ill-humour left him quickly, as sometimes happened, and he smiled, suddenly indulgent. "Oh, very well. I know you are keen to see the amateur antics yourself! Let's join the merry throng."

Joey laughed, pleased that he wasn't going to be disagreeable.

They managed to find seats well to the front of the hall. The back seats were occupied by the young men, with the girls immediately in front of them. A considerable amount of noise, talking, scuffling, and laughter, came from this quarter. Joey, glancing round, was amused to see Arthur happily seated just behind the young teacher from Aestervoe.

The lamps were removed from the hall, the curtains swung back, and the audience fell silent, except for a few piercing whistles from the more exuberant occupants of the back seats. Throughout each act, the children sat entranced. Caro knew that the sole ambition of her life would be to perform on that stage. She spent the time between items contemplating what her role might be. She had acted in school plays, and recited, but she thought she would like to sing. Like the young woman who had sung *Little Sir Echo*. (Caro's singing was enthusiastic, rather than tuneful.)

Marina preferred the short sketches. She liked the funny costumes and the beards which kept slipping about on the wearers' faces. She didn't understand why the dialogue was funny, but it must be, for people kept laughing, so she joined in, a little behind everyone else. Connie's expression of enjoyment was muted by her placid, undemonstrative nature, but she applauded each performance with soft slaps of her plump hands.

It was during the interval that Joey discovered that Hugh's sisters were seated just behind. She turned to greet them and received cool little nods in return. She wondered why they were always so standoffish, and decided that, as Kirsty would put it, it was "just their way."

May and Belle made very little attempt at conversation. Joey felt that she was chattering too much, and yet she had to make some sort of friendly overture. Not over-talkative by nature, she felt the strain of it. Would it always be the same, she wondered? Even after she and Hugh were married? Probably she wouldn't see much of them. And she couldn't, honestly, feel sorry about that.

The concert ended and everyone began to move towards the exit. The children were squeezed and jostled by the crowd but, through a gap, Caro caught a glimpse of some familiar figures standing by the door of the ladies' cloakroom, presumably waiting for the hall to be cleared and the dance to begin.

Caro nudged Connie and they peered round the back of the fat woman immediately in front of them, trying to get a better view. The 'big girls' stood in a row, close to each other, backs to the wall, in more senses than one. They were wide-eyed, solemn-faced, and more than a little lost-looking. Their plain, schoolgirlish frocks bore no resemblance to the creations they had described.

The little girls looked at the big girls. Somehow, they didn't look such very big girls, after all.

Chapter 4

A VISIT TO WASTERVOE

JANUARY crept past, each day bringing interminable gales and rain. The children were given half-days off school but, used to the short northern days of winter, amused themselves happily enough indoors, playing with 'paper folk', and doll's houses improvised from shoe-boxes. Later on, these half-days would have to be made up for the school had to show a specific number of openings on the register, but all that was in a vague and distant future. In the meantime, it was good to play in the comfortable living-room, with Tammas blinking at them from his seat on the hearth, the gale shrieking round the house, booming in the chimney and rattling the doors, while an apprehensive Kirsty peered out through the dark windows and expressed the hope that "everything would stand."

The following month brought snow, but not too much. Every afternoon, after school, the girls sledged on the fields which ran down to the burn until the light faded and they came in to tea with rosy faces and frozen fingers and toes.

Hugh went south to rejoin his ship. The house of Hivdalea still stood untouched. The night before he'd left, he and Joey had looked over it again. Hugh was still full of plans for its conversion, adding more and more innovations to those already contemplated, and talking of "grants" and "loans". Joey had been non-committal, understanding none of it. When things needed to be done at Grinda Garth, Magnie, Davie, and even Arthur, turned to with hammers and nails and saws, and it was done. Presumably, that wasn't how Hugh worked.

March was a sunny month, with cold winds chasing cotton-wool clouds across a sky of periwinkle-blue. The girls, under Arthur's supervision, began to make kites. The table seemed to be perpetually covered with brown paper, pieces of thin wood, lengths of string, and torn newspapers to tie into the tails, as bigger and bigger kites evolved.

As it approached the time of the full moon, the high tides began, with correspondingly low ebbs which brought up wide stretches of sand beyond the stony beaches. The pier, where the goods for the shop were landed, was completely high-and-dry, and it was possible to walk along the beach to Wastervoe, instead of round by the road, shortening the journey considerably.

Sometimes, Joey would go shopping in Wastervoe, which boasted five shops, and one bright and blowy Saturday she decided to make the trip, taking Caro with her. Connie had a cold, and a chagrined Marina was also left behind because her six-year-old legs might tire on the journey.

Joey carried a square basket, with a lid, on her back, by means of a length of rope which went across her shoulders and the top of her chest. In it reposed her week's work; a Fair Isle pullover which she would sell at one or other of the shops in order to buy the groceries.

As they walked along the beach below the Aestervoe shop, they saw Arthur rolling barrels of paraffin into the store and waved to him as they went past. Ahead of them, the sand stretched, glistening wet, its flatness shortening the distance deceptively.

Reaching the Wastervoe side of the voe, they clambered up onto the withered grass then took the track leading up past the bakery. The door stood open and there was an appetising scent of new-baked bread. After the walk in the fresh, sea-air, both Joey and Caro felt a little hungry. In the low shed at the side, the bakery engine was giving out its slow, dull beat, and little puffs of smoke issued from a pipe sticking out through the wall.

There weren't many customers in the shop Joey chose to patronise first. She was escorted into the back-shop where the knitwear was bought by the shop-keeper, a middle-aged man, tall and portly, with his watch-chain straddling his brown waistcoat.

Caro was left in the outer shop to wait. She leaned against the polished wooden counter, breathing in the assorted fascinating smells of salt fish, rubber boots, linoleum, new loaves, and moth-balls and sulphur from the wool on the shelves. Her gaze lingered on the bottles of sweets. Before setting out, her grandfather had given her tuppence and Kirsty had contributed a penny. Three whole pennies; it was a good lot of money.

A bell tinkled above the door as people went in and out, and sometimes a draught of wind would set the tin pails, hanging in clusters from the ceiling, clanging like an echo.

She wandered over to the short side-counter and found a stand full of Donald M'Gill postcards. She spent an enthralling ten minutes perusing them; the fat ladies in red bathing-costumes, the under-nourished young men with droopy moustaches, and the glamorous girls with fox-furs, red nails, and cigarette holders.

Joey came back at last and Caro went to stand beside her and watch what she bought. She also had to decide what she herself would buy with her three precious pennies. She looked towards the sweetie shelf but her view was slightly obscured by a large cut-out of a woman's head covered with hairnets.

When everything had been packed into the basket, Joey said, "Now, you have some money to spend, haven't you? And we must take something back for Connie and Marina. What do you think they'd like?"

In the end, they bought Lucky Bags. The sweets in Lucky Bags weren't all that good, tiny coloured morsels of scented sweetness, but this was compensated for by the excitement of wondering what the gift inside would be. Caro, because she had a penny left over, also bought a stick of rock, pink, with a ring on the end.

Joey asked if she could leave her basket in the shop and collect it later. As soon as they were outside, Caro demanded to know where they were going next.

"Is it to another shop, Joey? The one where they sell frocks and hats and things?" She would enjoy seeing the cotton dresses and blouses hanging round the walls and maybe Joey would buy something for her.

But Joey shook her head. "I must go and see Hugh's mother and father. I haven't been for long enough."

"Oh," Caro wasn't sure she would like that. She hadn't been to Hugh's home before, nor met his parents, and the prospect was not pleasing. She didn't like May and Belle.

The Sutherlands' house was a more superior dwelling than the croft houses round about. It had two bay windows and a glass porch; its paintwork was fresh and the doorstep spotlessly white. Everything about it, both outside and in, was scrupulously clean. Even the flower-beds, bare though they were at present, were as exact as if they had been measured out, and the fuchsia hedge had been thoroughly disciplined.

Inside, although everything was shining with cleanliness, the decor was gloomy. The solid Edwardian furniture, gleaming with polish, took up almost every inch of space in the room, and the large pictures, in their heavy, ornate frames, had darkened over the years so that in some cases it was difficult to distinguish what they represented. It was a room of unimaginative affluence; substantial, and claustrophobic.

Belle had opened the door, polite but cool, as always, her smile scarcely more than a quirk of her thin lips. May was away for a few days, she told Joey, and her mother was upstairs, resting, but her father was "turning over the vegetable plot." She would go and tell him that Joey had called.

Ushered into the sitting-room, they sat down on the green plush chairs. Caro's feet dangled in mid-air and Joey, too, looked oddly uncomfortable, perched on the edge of her chair as if ready for flight. The clock on the bottom shelf of the over-mantel ticked with a sonorous, dignified sound. It appeared to be the only sound to be heard throughout the whole house.

Caro found herself alternately attracted and repelled by the huge glass case of stuffed birds and small animals which took up at least half of one wall. An eagle grasped its prey – a rabbit – in sharp talons; a weasel wrapped itself round a tree-stump; a drab frog crouched on a stone; and in every conceivable space in-between, birds of varying shapes and sizes perched on uncertain foot-holds. Fur and feathers had a dusty, lifeless look, but the eyes glittered with an unblinking, intense virulence, unlikely in a living creature. No matter where she looked, Caro found her gaze drawn back to the case and its immovable occupants.

Before Belle returned with her father, the door opened and old Mrs Sutherland came in. She was a woman of average height but so fat that she appeared to be short. Her eyes, nose, and mouth, were almost lost in the rolls of fat which creased her face. She was dressed entirely in black and moved with incredible slowness across the polished linoleum.

"Oh – I hope you didn't get up just because of us ..." Joey began, and pulled nervously at the belt of her coat for, somehow, she could not feel at home in this house, not even when Hugh was there.

Mrs Sutherland sat down in one of the armchairs by simply falling backwards into it. "Oh no, my dear, I'd have been getting up anyway, in ten minutes or so. I heard you come in, and we have very few visitors."

She gave a wheezy sigh, smiled at Caro by compressing her tiny mouth and, from somewhere in her voluminous garments, produced a couple of caramels for her.

Hugh's father was a heavily-built man. Hugh would be very like him in a few years time. He had an easy smile, and a hearty, bluff manner which made Caro respond to him. He was, at heart, fond of children, and went out of his way to make a fuss of Caro and draw her into the conversation.

Joey watched, a little surprised, and couldn't help comparing Belle and May with their parents. Mr Sutherland, so open and friendly, his wife dull, but kindly. Yet the daughters were so cool and aloof. Even Hugh had a certain stiffness of manner at times, she had to admit.

Old Mr Sutherland couldn't do enough to entertain the child. He produced a music-box which played *Drink to Me Only*, and a toy where a small wooden man went up a ladder, entered a tiny windmill, came out again and down the ladder, but now he was carrying a sack. It was rather young for Caro, but she was interested, wondering what happened inside the little windmill.

When it was time to leave, Mrs Sutherland decreed that Caro was to have an orange and an apple from the dish on the sideboard, and a sour-faced Belle complied.

Caro received the gift with obvious pleasure. Fruit was a rare luxury, usually reserved for Christmas.

Joey collected her basket from the shop and they began to walk back home across the beach. There was a smoky-blue haze to the hills, and a mackerel sky; pale-blue overlaid with wrinkly cloud of dove-grey, and a lemon glow in the west. Here and there, on the wet sand, dark silhouettes walked slowly, bending from the waist and peering down at the sand, watching for the tell-tale spurt of water which would indicate the presence of razor-fish.

"On Monday, if the ebb is big again, I'll have to try for some spoots for our tea," commented Joey, using the local name for the razor-fish.

"I could come with you," said Caro, a little wistfully. She would love to try to catch a spoot herself, but she knew she wouldn't be allowed to. Often, she would go down to the big ebb with Connie and Marina and always Kirsty would admonish.

"Now, don't you go after spoots. You'll only lay your hands open on the shells!"

The light was beginning to fade by the time they reached home. In contrast to the Sutherlands' impeccable house, the Grinda Garth living-room seemed shabby and none too tidy. But the warmth of the open fire was pleasant after the chilly spring air and the tea, wholesome and filling, was already on the table.

The visit to the Sutherlands had been interesting but, on the whole, Caro thought, it was more comfortable to live at Grinda Garth. Joey's thoughts were running on much the same lines.

Chapter 5

STARTING THE VOAR

IT WAS a day in early April. Joey rinsed out the muslin cloth which was used for straining the milk and went out to hang it on the fence. The morning sun threw down beams of light which turned into liquid gold where they touched the firth, out to the south-east. Somewhere, high in the pale sky, a lark was bubbling with song, its wings a blur.

The chimneys of Leabakka were silhouetted darkly against the jewel-blue of the firth and, to the north of the house, behind the byre, a line of washing swayed gently in the light breeze. Charlotte had been early at her wash-tub.

Joey sighed, and turned back towards the open door of Grinda Garth. In the barn, Kirsty was cutting the last of the seed potatoes and, on the green at the top of the fields Magnie was preparing to harness Pride and Peggie, the two working-mares, to the plough. Today, they were 'starting the voar', beginning the work of the croft that would continue throughout the summer and into the autumn until it ended with the lifting of the potatoes in October.

Joey had never cared for the work of the croft but it was a necessary evil. This morning, she had awoken with the lowness of spirits that an unpleasant task evokes. Adding to her despondency was the fact that the previous day she had had a short letter from May Sutherland. May and Belle were to visit relatives in the town and May was to have a fitting for her bridesmaid's dress. Perhaps Joey would consider going with them?

Joey had spent a restless night, wondering if she could possibly get away for even a couple of days. They had distant cousins in Lerwick with whom Kirsty exchanged some half-dozen or so letters in the course of the year, for the affiliation of kinship was strong in the older generation. Probably they would be willing to put her up. Anyway, she would wait until the following day before replying to May's note.

In the living-room she found Arthur, on hands and knees, searching under the restin-shair for his rubber boots, and looking as morose as she felt. He had managed to get the day off from the shop to help with the laying-in of the potatoes, being more fortunate than Davie who had had to go to work as usual, as days off weren't easily come by when one worked for 'the County'. Arthur, however, scarcely regarded himself in a fortunate light; in common with most young people, he had little use for the hard grind of the croft.

"It looks as if it's going to stay dry, at least," said Joey, in an attempt to lighten the gloom.

"Yes – worse luck!" came Arthur's muffled reply.

"Nina is coming over to help, and likely Willa will come up, too. Auntie Kirsty is expecting her, anyway." After all, Willa and Tom got their year's supply of potatoes from Grinda Garth. "And the bairns will help when the school comes out, at least, Connie and Caro will."

Arthur's ill-humour didn't allow him to find any bright side to the situation. He hauled on his boots and went, stamping over the green towards his father.

Kirsty came bustling in, her old brown shawl folded over her head and round her black coat, her hands dusty from the potatoes, and began to collect buckets and basins to hold the seed. Soon afterwards, Nina arrived, smiling, pleased to be having a day out, even if it was a working-holiday.

But it was pleasant to work out in the sunshine. They were lucky to get such a day, Kirsty said. She had seen plenty of days when they had had to shelter from sleety showers, crouching with sacks over their heads, in the middle of a muddy rig, and the hail-puckles rattling round their fingers.

The sacks of seed potatoes stood at the top of the field and, from them, they filled their utensils. Each one took a portion of the field to plant, in a row from top to bottom. Joey and Nina had intended to work next to each other, then they could have enjoyed a little light-hearted conversation with all the latest gossip, but they were thwarted by Willa who, somehow, managed to station herself between them like some gloomy duenna.

Magnie set in the plough at the top of the rig. The mares plodded down the slope, led by Arthur for the first furrow, which turned over behind them, glistening brown. Soon the gulls arrived, hopefully following the plough for the worms which would be turned up.

Nina started a conversation with Arthur when he came to work at her other side. From time to time, Joey caught Nina's light laugh. Arthur was looking a little more cheerful now. She tried to concentrate on Willa's tedious discourse, delivered in a voice that was slightly breathless from bending.

"… and you'll have heard about Tom's cousin, Jemima Johnson, that was married to a Brown man from Lynna Isle, and he met with an accident last year, fell in the hold of his ship and never rose more, and now she's in the Sanatorium …"

Joey cast her mind back, trying to recall what she had heard of these relations of Tom's, people she had never met. "Hasn't she got a small daughter? About Marina's age?"

Willa nodded. "And a boy, he's younger, maybe about two. There's some neighbour looking after them … if you're going up to fill your bucket you may as well take mine with you. It'll save my legs."

Magnie had turned the plough at the bottom of the field and was coming back up. He held the plough so that it didn't cut into the ground, but here and there a sharp scar indicated that he was not completely successful. As the horses passed, Joey felt their warm, pungent smell, and Peggie, who was the less placid of the two, blew down her nose and rolled a limpid eye.

When Joey returned, Willa continued her monologue where she had left off, the theme prominently death, disease, and disaster. "… and old Leebie Manson passed away, and I hear there's cousins from over at West Hamar coming to clear up her things and have a displenishing sale …"

Kirsty, who was on her way up to the house to make the 'twal', overheard Willa's remark, and paused. "Poor body, there was never one of her own who looked to her when she was living but there'll be more dogs than bones now, if they think there's any pickings to be had." Kirsty snorted, rather as Peggie had done. She added, sardonically, "Well, I hope it sets them up!" and continued on her way.

For a moment, Joey let her mind dwell on old Leebie who had lived in one room on the end of the shop store. A tiny, dark room, crammed to bursting point with rickety furniture and all sorts of knick-knacks and ornaments. If her relatives had avoided her, her friends had more than made up for it, for her kindliness and generosity with what little she had, had caused her to be well-liked in Aestervoe. Joey had often popped in to see Leebie when she had been shopping. In a small place like Aestervoe, one person's passing made a void and the place was that much poorer.

At three o'clock, the children arrived home from school and, in high glee, Caro and Connie found pails and prepared to lay-in. Marina trailed behind the plough, picking up the pieces of broken glass and crockery that was thrown up. Once, she had heard a story of how someone had found a gold ring, and she didn't see why she shouldn't find something of value, too, perhaps not a gold ring, but it would be good even to find a sixpence, a penny, even.

After about an hour, the enthusiasm of Caro and Connie began to subside, and they began to take longer and longer over the filling of their buckets, and then Willa, too, took herself off "to see to Tom's tea."

"You'll be working for a while after tea, I suppose," said Nina. "I'll stay on …"

"I don't know," Joey straightened her back. Her muscles were beginning to ache. "Uncle Magnie may think that the mares have done enough for one day."

"I can't work any longer, anyhow," said Arthur, "I've got something else on."

Standing in the furrow behind him, Caro and Marina began to giggle, while a slow smile crossed Connie's face. He looked at them suspiciously.

"What's so funny?"

They went on giggling. "We know something," Caro said, cheekily.

"We know something you don't know," said Connie, not to be out-done.

Arthur, despite his twenty-five years, had neither the maturity nor sense of humour to treat the children's teasing with indifference. He suspected that they had heard something, probably at school, and immediately connected it with his inability to make progress with the new teacher.

"It's to do with Miss Isbister," hinted Caro, confirming his worst suspicions, and moving further up the field, out of his range. Connie followed, pressing her fingers to her mouth and giggling even more.

Arthur took a couple of steps towards them, his brows drawn down, grimly determined that they should not get the better of him.

"If you would ignore them, Arthur, they'd leave you alone," advised Joey. She gave Nina a rueful look and shook her head. "He can't see that they want to get him mad, just for the fun of it."

"Do you think they've really heard anything?" said Nina.

"More than likely they'll have heard that he's running after their teacher. You know what bairns are, especially the older girls. Anyway, he isn't the only one!"

At the bottom of the rig, Kirsty pushed the last piece of seed-potato into the damp earth and then stood up. With a dusty hand, she shaded her eyes and peered towards the slowly-setting sun. It was almost directly above the dip in the hills behind Wastervoe; time she was getting the tea underway. She walked over to the grass at the side of the rig and began to clean her boots, scraping them vigorously amongst the coarse tussocks, and singing under her breath.

Kirsty only ever sang two songs. She had no musical talent whatever and the melodies to both were similarly untuneful and delivered in a series of short puffs and gasps. The words consisted of one phrase repeated over and over again. One song was used when her work required quick, energetic movements, and she would gasp out, "*When we all get married we'll have sausages for tea.*" Now, as she began to ascend the slope, slowly, hands clasped on her back, she was singing her other song, "*... and I rise content in the morning abune sweet Rothesay Bay.*"

The children ran after her, hoping for a pre-tea snack. The fun was over now, for Arthur had an extra part of the rig to do now that Kirsty had left. It wasn't long before Marina was back to announce that their grandfather could start to unyoke the mares for the tea was nearly ready.

Joey and Nina collected the buckets and then wandered up towards the house, taking their time.

The sun was setting fast now. On the hills to the west, the old heather was being burned and the smoke drifting down towards the voe. There was a row of little fires in a diagonal line up the hill and a blue haze lay over the western landscape. The woody, tangy scent was strong in the air.

Nina went into the porch, where Kirsty was pouring milk into the big jug with the blue rim, while Joey paused for a moment outside the door to glance at the garden. The daffodils seemed late this spring and the willow, still bare of buds, threw a delicate tracery of slender branches against a mother-of-pearl sky of greys and soft peach.

Joey sighed with weariness and went indoors. Though she ached in every bone, there was a satisfaction in knowing that a necessary job had been done. The perplexing problem of May Sutherland's letter had been relegated to the back of her mind but she now knew what her answer would be. She couldn't leave Grinda Garth now, not when they had started the voar.

Chapter 6

'FASHION PLATES'

CARO slouched in her seat, staring gloomily down at the top of her desk. With her pencil, she added a mast and sail to the boat already drawn beside the ink-well, scoring deeply into the wood, then added her initials – C.C.M. – Caroline Catherine Mouat.

All around her there was the silence of the classroom, broken from time to time by a sigh or the muttered calculations of a troubled mathematician. She drew two moon-faces, printing 'Willa' underneath one and 'miss I' under the other, then the point of her pencil snapped off. The sound seemed to her like a pistol shot in the stillness.

"Caroline Mouat!" Miss Isbister's voice cut sharply through the restless silence. "Have you finished your work?"

"No, Miss." Caro opened her history book at random and relieved her feelings by dipping the broken pencil into the ink-well and adding a pipe, moustache, and glasses to the picture of Joan of Arc. There might be trouble about it later, if it was discovered, but as she was already in Miss Isbister's black-books, a bit more trouble would be neither here nor there.

She crouched lower, hiding behind the broad back of Matthew Goudie at the desk in front, and stole a covert look round the room. In the row of desks nearest the wall, Connie was laboriously stitching at a pair of white cotton knickers that looked enormous. The white was marred at intervals by tiny red spots for Connie's needle pierced her fingers almost as often as it did the material. In the front row Marina, amongst the other infants, was crayoning in her drawing-book with much vigour and blowing of crayon-dust. There was a yellowish patch on her chin and her hands were almost entirely blue.

The top class was doing arithmetic but everyone else was having drawing, or hand-work, or silent reading, something of a relaxing nature. Everyone except Caro, who had been caught in the dreadful act of dropping inky pellets of blotting-paper down the back of Ella Flaws' blouse.

And it had been Ella's fault entirely, yet she had been allowed to do raffia-work while Caro had been moved to a seat nearer the front where Miss Isbister could "keep an eye on her," and given the task of learning rows of dates to be heard at the end of afternoon school. It wasn't fair!

She caught Ella's self-satisfied smile, and stuck out her tongue, then glanced hastily towards Miss Isbister. Fortunately, the teacher was bending over the work of one of the artistic infants who had just marched out to the table, proudly bearing his masterpiece.

In her ears, Caro could still hear Ella's complacent voice. "Miss Isbister is coming to our house tonight. Harry is bringing her on his motorbike." Harry was Ella's grown-up brother. "She likes Harry. She likes him better than your Uncle Arthur. Arthur Mouat is just a foolish youth, my mother says!"

Whatever Caro's private opinion of Arthur might be, to belittle him was to insult the family. Too furious to find words, it was then that she had manufactured the pellets and popped them down the back of Ella's pink cotton blouse.

Miss Isbister was pinning up the infant's effort on the wall, just below the big green map of China; a crimson ship on a royal-blue sea, with a cloud of black smoke coming out of its yellow funnel. The small glass clock on the teacher's table went very slowly, but Caro knew that she would never memorise those dates in time. She knew, too, that she would be told to learn them over the weekend with, perhaps, some more added on. Why couldn't they have Miss Isbister to her tea at Grinda Garth? Then she would be able to get away with anything, just like Ella Flaws!

But at last they were free, and it was Friday! Back home, at Grinda Garth, the girls hung their school-bags on the hook behind the closet door.

Marina said, "We had a good time at school today, drawing, all afternoon. I drew a house and a garden and a woman with a big round skirt, like the one on Joey's pin-cushion."

"All right for you," Caro said, unguardedly. "I got hundreds of silly dates to learn, and I couldn't, and now I've got to do them for Monday, and extra ones, as well."

"It was your own fault," said Connie, placidly aware that no fault could have been found with her own conduct.

"Oh, and what way was that?" asked Kirsty, who was cleaning a lamp-glass with a piece of crumpled paper, turning it round and round against the smoke-stains.

"Caro was playing-up in the school today," Connie informed her. "Miss Isbister was mad at her."

Caro's face flamed. "Connie, you told on me!"

Connie had the grace to look a little shame-faced.

"I thought you went to your school to learn, not to carry on tomfoolery," Kirsty said. "It's changed days since I was at the school. Then-a-days, we had to walk to Wastervoe, carrying our peat for the fire with us."

"That was an awful long way to go," said Caro, anxious to keep her grandmother off the subject of her own misdemeanours, "especially in winter."

"Oh, we didn't go all that often in the winter-time, not unless the weather was fine, and dependable."

Marina's eyes grew round. "But didn't they put you in prison? That's what happens if you don't go to the school. Jessie Robertson's mother told her that. Jessie sits in the desk with me. Jessie doesn't want to come to the school."

Kirsty was shaking her head. "It was different, then-a-days. We weren't forced to go – it wasn't – what do they call it, now – it wasn't compulsory. We only went if we wanted to."

The children stared at her. "And did anyone *ever* go?" asked Connie.

"Oh yes, most of the bairns went."

"You mean you walked all that way because you wanted to go?" asked Caro, incredulously.

"That's right. Of course, our father was very keen for us to learn to read and write and do our counts, but we would likely have gone of our own accord, anyway. It was better than staying at home to struggle and work on the croft all day, though we had our fair share of that, all the same." Kirsty breathed on the lamp-glass, then rubbed it up with an old rag.

The girls asked no more questions. It was incomprehensible that anyone could actually want to attend school. They could only think that it must have been awful different in the olden days!

Kirsty peered at the lamp-glass, saw no more marks on it, and replaced it firmly inside the little metal points which surrounded the wick. It was a pretty lamp, with a fount of pink glass decorated with a painted nosegay of deeper pink flowers, and set on a shiny black stand. Kirsty picked it up carefully and walked towards the door of the ben-end.

The ben-end was a sittingroom-cum-spare-bedroom. Behind the door stood the bed, an iron framework with brass knobs, and a starched, white valance which went all the way round to hide the legs, and which Kirsty called a 'pawn'. Not only did it hide the legs but also the various boxes stored under the bed; the box, for instance, holding Kirsty's Sunday hat; and the one containing the Japanese tea-set, carefully packed in tissue-paper, which Magnie had brought home for Kirsty when he had been going to sea, and they had been courting.

In the corner opposite the bed there was a wardrobe of polished mahogany and, under the window, a sofa with a carved back, upholstered in red moquette. Above the fireplace was placed the gem of Kirsty's worldly possessions – an over-mantel, reaching almost to the ceiling. It had a large, bevelled mirror in the centre and several smaller mirrors down each side, interspersed with little shelves supported on tiny ornamental pillars. On the shelves were displayed the treasures of a life-time: shells, and bits of coral from more exotic shores; a set of ebony elephants; a collection of circular boxes, one fitting inside the other, and ringed in red, yellow, and black; a hideous pink vase with gold and silver flocking.

On either side of the imitation-copper fender which enclosed the hearth-stone stood two shell-cases, relics of the 1914-18 War, polished so that the fire-light glittered in them. Kirsty kept her various knitting-needles in one.

Against the back wall stood a circular table, with one central leg, ending in three carved feet. The top had a design in inlaid wood and across it lay a fringed runner of Indian silk. Kirsty put the lamp down in the centre of it.

Caro's eyes took in the newly-whitened sides of the chimney and the new, gold-coloured taffeta quilt on the bed. "Is somebody coming?" she asked.

"Oh, Joey is having some of the lasses in." Kirsty glanced round the room to make sure that nothing had been left undone.

Caro, who had as great a zest for gossip as her Great-aunt Charlotte, would have liked to be able to sneak into the room, unobserved, later on. Joey didn't like anyone else in the room when she had visitors. They would knit, and giggle, and stop talking as soon as anyone opened the door.

"Where is Joey?" Caro asked.

"She went down to the shop to get in her provender," replied Kirsty, giving a twitch to the brown chenille curtains.

"Oh! Can I go to meet her?"

"That can you," Kirsty readily gave permission. "She'll maybe need somebody to give her a hand, for she had to take the flask for paraffin, though maybe she'll leave that for Arthur to bring home."

Caro rushed through to the living-room, her feet clattering on the linoleum. Connie was there, searching in the cupboard for something to eat.

"We can go to meet Joey from the shop. Where's Marina?"

"Gone to the hill-stack with Daa."

Caro remembered seeing their grandfather and Marina go past the ben window, Magnie with the kishie for peats slung across his shoulder.

By the time she and Connie reached the shop, they still hadn't met Joey. It was a 'goods' day and the shop was crowded right to the door. The girls passed the time by looking in the window and, when that no longer amused them, they wandered round the building and stared at the 'big house' where the shopkeeper lived.

It was an awful big house for just two people, they considered. It was easily the most important-looking house in the village, with its bay-windows and the porch with the serrated top and the green-painted garden-seat in front. Surprisingly, the seat had two occupants. The girls couldn't remember seeing anyone actually sitting there before.

The two got up and began to walk over the grass towards the shop and Caro and Connie saw that they were what they termed 'big girls'. But what caused the girls to stare in open-mouthed amazement was that they were wearing trousers! Wide-legged, navy-blue trousers! None of the girls or women on the island wore trousers. By the time Caro and Connie had accompanied

Joey home, Caro's greatest ambition was to own a pair of trousers.

As Joey unpacked her basket, she casually mentioned the two strangers. "I saw the two girls who are on holiday at the Garriocks'. They're from the town, a cousin's daughters, or something."

Kirsty nodded. "They went walking out the road this morning when I was down at Willa's. A right pair of fashion plates! They were wearing breeks!"

Joey laughed. "Slacks!"

"Whatever they call them they just look like breeks to me!" Kirsty replied.

In the bustle of clearing-up after tea, nobody paid much attention to the whereabouts of the children. Kirsty had broken a cup and Marina had salvaged the pieces and carried them off to supplement the crockery at the play-house, in the shelter of the byre. If anyone had thought about it, they would have assumed that the children were all there together.

But Caro and Connie were upstairs in their grandparents' bedroom. In the space below the window, there was a chest where Kirsty hoarded all sorts of unwanted garments in the belief that someday "they would come in handy." As Caro raised the lid there was an over-powering smell of moth-balls.

"There's sure to be something in here," she said. "They were wide, those slacks, so it won't matter if they seem a bit on the big side." She felt that if only she could wear a pair of slacks she wouldn't mind about Ella Flaws or all those dates which had to be learned. Wearing slacks, she would learn them all the better.

She came upon an old pair of navy serge trousers belonging to her father, very shiny at the knees, which had been kept for the dirty jobs which cropped up from time to time, such as the tarring of the roof. She picked up the scissors, docked off the legs at what she considered an appropriate length, and handed the trousers to Connie.

"You can have those."

Kirsty's chest didn't appear to hold much in the way of trousers. There were dresses, blouses, and some old blankets intended to be used for the inside of a quilt, but there seemed to be only one other pair of trousers, grey, with a white pin-stripe. Caro cut them down to size, in an uneven line, and donned them, using the belt of her gym-frock to secure them at the waist.

She drew in a breath of satisfaction. "I bet they look fine. Let's go downstairs now."

"Yes," agreed Connie, and added, "but you go first."

Arthur, preparing to go out for the evening, emerged from the small bedroom behind the stairs which he shared with Davie. Kirsty looked up from putting the cutlery into the table-drawer and observed the best jacket with the half-belt at the back, and the new, brown and white sports shoes.

"You've got your go-ashores on, I see, " she remarked, dryly. "You'll be wearing spats next!"

"Spats!" Arthur said, disdainfully, "no one wears spats nowadays. I've had to put on these awful old flannels again. I wish you would find time to alter those new ones I bought months ago, Mam."

Caro and Connie made their entrance. Kirsty gave them one grim look.

"You're not wearing that rubbish and folk coming in. Upstairs and take it off as quick as ever it went on."

"It's slacks, not rubbish," defended Caro. "It's the fashion."

"Upstairs, my lady, and no more about it!"

Arthur gave a cry of anguish. "My new flannels!" He made a grab for Caro who eluded him and dashed back up the stairs as fast as her flapping trouser-legs would allow.

"Mam!" he appealed to Kirsty, "Do you see what they've done? My new flannels, never been on! What are you going to do about that?"

"Not much I can do, my bairn. Now the deed is done."

She began to chuckle, as the vision of Caro disappearing up the stairs in a flurry of grey flannel crossed her mind. "Anyway," she added, between gasps, "you'll have no need to complain now that you didn't get them shortened!"

Chapter 7

WILLA'S BOMBSHELL

MAY, which had come in showery and cold, had settled down into the type of weather usually associated with that month; calm, moist, and misty. The drifts of mist had come in from the south-east and the sun had the appearance through it of a silver button, while the hills took on varying shades of hazy blue. Lapwings were beginning to nest in the field to the north of Grinda Garth and their calls came eerily out of the mist. Down at the shore, the wild duck gave sporadic cries, plaintive or querulous, as they deemed necessary.

Nina came over to Grinda Garth visiting one evening, together with Alexina Hoseason, the youngest of the five sisters who lived at Houll, the house on the headland. Nina was pleased because she had got a 'special' order from the shop for an all-over Fair Isle jumper.

"A forty-two chest," she said with simulated dejection. "Nobody ought to be as big as that!" But she was pleased, all the same; the larger the garment, the more money she could expect.

Alexina, who had buck teeth and glasses, but a ready smile, produced her knitting, a bordered cardigan – plain, with a pattern just above the basque.

They didn't go into the ben-end, as Joey's visitors usually did, for there was no one else in the house. Instead, they all three settled down in the living-room. Magnie and Davie were planting the corn; Magnie sowing, while Davie went behind, leading Pride who was drawing the harrow. In the northern side of the garden, Kirsty was setting cabbage plants which had been grown from seed in the planti-crub at the foot of the rigs, down by the burn. She was well-protected from the damp air, in her old working coat and the brown shawl over her head and shoulders. Her hands were folded on her back as she scuffled first one foot, then the other, through the soft earth, making two long gullies for the plants.

At the gable-end of the byre, the children were amusing themselves at the play-house, propping up bits of old crockery on the wooden box which represented the dresser. Marina was putting buttercups into a jam-jar to decorate the table which was a piece of wood balanced on two stones. Connie was making a cake from earth and dock-seed. Caro was apparently on a shopping expedition, gathering small stones into a paper-bag and holding an animated conversation with an imaginary shop-assistant.

Joey smiled, as she watched them through the window, then let the curtain fall into place again. It was advisable to keep an eye on their goings-on! She fetched her own knitting and joined Nina and Alexina round the fire. The conversation turned on recent and forth-coming events.

"Are you coming to the dance after the roup on Friday, Joey?" Nina asked. "I hope it'll keep dry but with this misty weather you can never be sure that it won't come a run of rain. If it does, I think it will be better to row across the voe instead of walking round by the road. What's your opinion?"

"I don't know – if I'll be going, I mean," said Joey. She was a little uncertain as to whether she ought to be going to dances as she was engaged and her fiance away.

"Oh, come on – what's the harm in that?" demanded Nina, forthright as usual. "You'll be with us."

"I suppose I might," Joey said, cautiously.

"Wouldn't it be fine to drive to a dance in a car?" said Alexina, speaking rather timidly as was her way. "You wouldn't get blown about, or wet, or your shoes get dirty ..."

"No, and that reminds me ..." Nina stopped knitting and leant forward, her eyes alight, her expression animated, "have you heard about the lodgers at the Spences'?"

"I heard there were two men there, something to do with the new telephone cable, and I saw a car standing at the gate, a yellow affair with a hood."

"One of them is about forty – he's married," Nina dismissed him. "The other one is about our age; he's the one who drives the car. His name is Cecil Porter."

"Have you seen them, then?"

"Only in passing, but I met Nell Spence in the Post Office and I asked about them," Nina admitted, cheerfully.

"I was at the Spences' the day they arrived," Alexina said. "They seemed quite friendly. The young one – Cecil – is fairly good-looking."

"There's your chance, then! Set your cap for him and you might get a lift to the roup dance," said Nina.

Alexina gave a half-laugh and bent her head over her knitting, looking a little pink. Nina stared at her for a moment, her mouth slightly open, and clearly wishing she hadn't said what she had. It looked as if Alexina had been rather taken with Cecil Porter!

The porch door opened and Tammas, the cat, came in, shaking beads of moisture from his fur, while Kirsty followed behind. She took off her shawl and flung it over the arm of the restin-shair.

"Och, I think I've done enough for one night," she remarked, opening the large safety-pin which fastened her coat at the waist. She greeted Nina and Alexina, "Well, lasses, it's fine you managed to come in a while. Has Joey made you any tea?"

"I was just going to, only I was waiting to see if Uncle Magnie and Davie were near to finishing." Joey picked up the kettle from the hearth and hung it on the hook, then used the long, iron tongs to set up the peat-embers beneath it.

"They're a piece off finishing yet, so I don't think we'll wait. They can come in for their tea and finish afterwards," said Kirsty. "And it's time the bairns were in, lying out in the damp night air, catching their deaths."

Joey went to call them. The play-house had lost none of its attraction and they came reluctantly, with some protest on the part of Caro and Marina and gloomy resignation from Connie. Their noses were red with cold, and Marina's hands were mottled blue, and damp to the touch.

"You've been playing with water again, Marina," Joey rebuked her. "Auntie Kirsty will be mad if she knows."

"It wasn't much water, Joey. Only what the jam-jar could hold," Marina excused herself.

"Oh, Marina! The cuffs of your coat are soaking!" As she helped the child off with her coat, Joey said to Caro, "Jump off and tell the men that their eight o'clock's is ready, will you?"

As she hung Marina's coat up behind the porch door, Joey hoped that it would dry off before Kirsty could discover the dampness of it. She was still young enough herself to hope that Marina wouldn't get into trouble and, besides, she didn't share Kirsty's conviction that wet hands could harm a healthy child, apart from a chilblain or two.

They had finished their tea, and Magnie and Davie had departed again to the rig, when Willa arrived. She seemed a little disconcerted at finding Nina and Alexina there.

"Oh, so you're here?" she remarked, without enthsiasm. "And what's your news?"

"Oh, everybody is going to the wall tonight," Nina replied, flippantly, her eyes glinting. She had no affection for her cousin Willa.

Willa, who had no sense of humour, took her at her word. "Mm, no doubt," she said, sourly.

"We were speaking about the roup," said Joey, saying the first thing that came into her mind in an effort to keep the peace.

Nina's lips quirked. "And the dance! And the two strangers at the Spences'. Is it not exciting to have a couple of strange men in the place?"

Willa sniffed. "You'd best keep clear of them. You know what south men are."

"No! I don't." Nina stared at Willa as if waiting to be enlightened.

Willa stared back, blinking pale, apathetic eyes. Then she turned to Kirsty, who had taken no part in the conversation but was searching through a bag containing scraps of wool in the hope of finding something suitable to darn a pair of Magnie's socks. There was a slight, enigmatic smile on Kirsty's face; it was impossible to know what she was thinking, or even if she had been listening to the conversation at all.

"Tom is off to Lynna Isle in the morning," Willa said. She obviously had more to say on this subject but she paused to give this first disclosure full impact, and await reactions. Kirsty obliged.

"That's surely sudden. I heard no word of it when I was down beside you this morning."

Willa gave a gusty sigh. "We had bad news this afternoon. You mind Tom's cousin Jemima, who was in the Sanatorium? She took a bad turn and died, suddenly. Tom thinks he would need to go and see to things. Her man had no relatives to speak of, just a couple of old aunts and some far-out cousins. Jemima was brought up in the house with Tom and his brothers, you know. He says she was just like a sister to them."

Kirsty was serious-faced now. She twisted the broad, gold wedding-ring round on her stumpy finger. "And what about the bairns? It's hard for them to lose their mother. And their father gone, too. They are the ones to be thought on, now."

"Tom thinks he'll have to bring them back with him, at least for the time-being," Willa divulged the rest of her news.

Kirsty accepted this without question. "He'll need to do that, seeing he's their nearest."

"It'll be a bit of an upheaval, I expect, two youngsters in the house," Willa pointed out. She had hoped for some remarks as to her kindness at taking in two orphans.

"Oh, there's only the two of you! It'll be lightsome, having some young life in the house," Kirsty assured her.

Willa rose to go, disappointed by the calm reception her news had been given, and the fact that no one seemed to think that she and Tom were doing anything out of the ordinary. They ought to have had some approbation from someone.

She put out a hand to open the porch door and encountered the wet sleeve of Marina's coat. "Tch, tch! Is this Marina's coat? It's soaking. Playing in the burn again, I suppose. If they were mine, I'd make sure they only needed one telling!"

"Let me see," Kirsty examined the coat, then turned back grimly to the living-room while Willa lingered in the doorway, a malevolent expression on her face.

Marina was subjected to the telling-off from which Joey had tried to shield her, and went sulkily to bed.

Nina and Alexina left, and Joey accompanied them, as was customary. At the end of the road, they took the grassy track up the headland towards Houll and then parted from Alexina at the yard-gate. From the headland, they could see the islands which lay in the firth, ethereal and indistinct in the misty haze, and the moon was high in the southern sky, a yellow blur behind the cloud. It was close on eleven o'clock, but still light.

Nina clutched Joey's arm and pointed back along the road. "Look! That must be Cecil Porter's car! Do you think he'll come as far as here?"

But the car stopped by the Spences' gate and the headlights went out. Nina gave an exclamation of disappointment.

Joey laughed. "Don't tell me you're enamoured of Cecil Porter, too?"

"Oh – well, not really!" Nina chuckled. "But he's someone new, a change from the same old faces. Besides, he's the only young man round here with a car. And what do you mean by 'too'?"

Joey had hoped that Nina wouldn't notice that slip of the tongue. It seemed unkind to discuss Alexina's all-too-apparent secret. She hesitated.

"You're thinking of Alexina?" said Nina. "Yes, if I had known about that beforehand I wouldn't have said what I did."

"I don't think there's anything – well, in it," Joey replied.

"Of course there isn't! Poor Alexina," Nina said, somewhat obscurely, but Joey knew that she was thinking that Alexina's romantic aspirations would soon be blighted. Alexina's was a colourless, timid personality. All the same, it didn't follow that Alexina was necessarily doomed to disappointment, stranger things had happened, and perhaps she would surprise them all yet.

"I'll come down the road with you, as far as the brig," said Nina.

At the little stone bridge, across the burn, they stood talking for a while, as young women do, of the things which interest them most. As the mist turned to a light drizzle, Joey said that they had better make for home.

"I won't come back up the road with you," she added, and Nina laughed.

"No, we mustn't be like the two old women who escorted each other backwards and forwards until the daylight came up!"

When Joey went up to bed that night, she found Marina still awake, and she bent to rearrange the heavy, home-quilt which was slipping off the bed.

"Aren't you asleep yet, dear? Would you like a drink, or something?"

"No, I was just thinking, Joey."

Joey hid a smile as she looked down at the small, unusually-solemn, face. "Oh! What about?"

"About Willa – I feel awful sorry for the little girl and boy who are going to live with her."

Joey did not rebuke her for the disparaging remark. How could she, she felt – when she found herself thinking the same?

Chapter 8

MEETING AT THE BURN

KIRSTY was walking down towards the burn, humming *Sweet Rothesay Bay* by fits and starts. It was a sunny morning, with a pale, violet-blue haze over the firth, and down by the burn the wild flowers were out. Marsh-marigolds laid a brilliant mantle over large areas, and Kirsty smiled, remembering how, once, when Joey had still been at school, she had asked Kirsty if that was what was meant by the 'field of the cloth of gold'. And although Kirsty had told her that she thought not, she had been as ignorant on the subject as the child.

Pale-pink milk-maids grew along the burn's edge, and clumps of wild iris with pointed leaves, almost waist-high, in the burn itself. On the other side, the rough, uncultivated ground which stretched up to Leabakka, was dotted with the white, fluffy heads of the bog-cotton. 'Cotton-plant', it was called, or 'Loki's Oo'.

Shading her eyes with her hand, Kirsty looked towards Leabakka and saw a thin plume of smoke rising from somewhere behind the byre. Charlotte was having a bonfire.

Kirsty turned her attention to the job in hand, which was to flit the two cows. She twisted Flekka's tether over her shoulder so that she could exert strength enough to haul the wooden stake out of the ground. Then, having moved the cow to better feeding-ground, she did the same for Bonnie. The job done, she was turning for home when she saw her sister, Charlotte, coming down the slope towards her. She waited, while Charlotte bobbed over the uneven ground and then crossed the burn, with an ungainly half-leap, at a narrow part.

With one accord, they found two dry tussocks, side-by-side, and sat down. "I was having a burning when I saw you, said Charlotte, stretching out her feet in their neat, black lacing-shoes, and smoothing the dark overall with its floral design down over the grey, cashmere stockings. "We got word that Johnny's ship docked on Tuesday. He has to work by the ship for a week, but he'll likely be home any time after that, so I'm doing a bit of clearing-out in the house."

"Yes, it all has to be done." Kirsty got into a more comfortable position and pushed back a hair-pin which had slipped out of one of her 'ear-muffs'. "Not that we've done much cleaning, so far, this year. I'm telling Arthur that he'll have to distemper the ceiling one of these nights, but he's not keen on that, as was only to be expected. He has to be out every night on some ploy of his own."

"The young ones are no' very anxious for work, no more than we were, I don't doubt. But it seems all the boys are going mad over this Isbister lass that's the teacher."

"Mm, she's a hard-sought woman," Kirsty said, caustically.

"I wonder who'll win the day, in the end?"

"No one round here, I'll be bound. She'll be after someone better than Aestervoe can offer."

Charlotte plucked a burra and began to chew on the end. "The school will be closing for the holidays. There'll be the prize-giving and a bit of a concert, likely? I like to go, to hear the bairns reciting and see the handwork and that. I hope it won't be on the day that I expect my chickens to start hatching out."

"Have you got a hen sitting, then?"

"That do I! Been sitting a week now. And a duck, as well."

"I would like to set a hen, this year. The half-a-dozen we have must be close on eight years old. We get eggs through the summer, but that's about the outside of it."

"My, you would need some young chickens to come into lay about February. I could give you a setting of eggs."

"That would be fine, but none of our hens are klokkin this year, so far."

"Mm – well, we just had the one that klokkit," Charlotte looked thoughtful. "But I believe I heard Mimie from Milbister saying she had a lot, couldn't get them to stop, so you'll be able to get one from her."

"I'll send the bairns over tonight, to see."

Charlotte began to laugh. "Speaking about the bairns – when I came over to Grinda Garth the other night, and passed them playing at their 'little house', do you know what they were doing? Playing at being the Sutherlands at Gardie Hill!"

"Oh, never speak!" Kirsty shook her head, torn between exasperation and amusement. "We've been subjected to that ever since Joey took Caro visiting there. Caro makes out she's Belle, and Connie has to be old Mrs Sutherland, while Marina is May …"

"Caro was giving out the orders as I came past, showing Connie how she should waddle, and wheeze. Then she was Belle receiving visitors – she's got that sour-faced creature to the life!" Charlotte paused, then added, "It's a mercy for Joey she's not going to live there. Is there any word when Hugh is coming home again?"

Kirsty was silent for a moment, picking naps off the sleeve of her woollen 'wearing' cardigan. "I thought maybe Joey had told Nina – I never know whether to speak or hold my tongue, when it's not my business, not that Joey would likely mind, but … well, the truth is, Charlotte, he isn't coming home this summer. Joey says he's wanting to go another trip for the sake of earning a bit of extra money …"

"Well, maybe that's for the best," Charlotte studied the tips of her shoes.

"Maybe. Anyway, there'll be no wedding this summer."

"I thought about saying something to Johnny, when I wrote to him, that it looked as if Joey might be wanting him for best-man, and then – I don't know why – but I decided I would never say anything ..." her voice trailed off.

"Likely it's selfish of me, but I'm no' wanting to lose Joey yet," Kirsty sighed, "though that day has to come."

Charlotte said, "How is Willa coping with the Brown bairns, do you think?"

"Oh, well enough, I would say, though it's early days yet. Willa was needing something to occupy herself with. Jem comes up to play with our bairns every day. Willa has all the work of Sydney, he's just two, but she seems very taken with him. They seem quiet bairns, so that's one blessing."

"I mind their mother, Jemima Johnson, when she was young and living with the Bains down at Setter. A quiet, mousy, little thing, she was. Do you mind hearing about her grandfather, old Barron Johnson? He was the meanest man in the parish, it was said. When he got married, he wouldn't buy a new suit, but wore the one he had had for his old aunt's funeral, and it hadn't been on his back in ten years. It was so tight, that when he began to dance the seams all gave way and he ended the night in his dungarees."

"There's been many a strange wedding. I'll not forget our cousin Willie's wedding, when the best-man mistook the date and had to be fetched seven miles in a horse-and-gig, and the bride and groom at the altar rails."

"That was John Davis Bairnson. His father was married four times, and he said he still had another flower to pluck!"

"Yea, but the Good Man plucked him first!" Kirsty said, dryly.

A light southerly breeze fanned past them, bringing the sweet scent of clover from the fields across the road, and a flock of young starlings, sable-coloured and fluffy, settled on the other side of the burn, poking with their beaks amongst the coarse grass, and squabbling.

Kirsty eyed the birds, watching their quick bursts of irascibility and shrieks of complaint. It seemed to remind her of something, for she drew her brows together and, turning to Charlotte, said, "Jessie Mary is coming in September. We had a letter yesterday."

Charlotte replied, with obvious relief, "We had our turn of her last year."

"I sometimes wonder why she bothers to come, for I'm sure it does her no good. She can't stand the bairns, and there's nothing but ructions," Kirsty sighed. "And as for Arthur – well, I'm glad when he keeps out of the way for I'm feared for what he might say to her."

"Och, it was the same beside us. She always had a nasty remark for Nina but, for a mercy, Nina never seems her."

"She's a trial, all the way of it, but what's to be done? I can't tell her not to come." Then, in self-reproach for any lack of charity she had shown, Kirsty added, "Poor body! She has none of her own, and no one caring about her."

"A lot of that is her own doing," Charlotte said, with candour.

Jessie Mary, a distant cousin, lived alone at Sandayre, a village on the west side of the island, but much of her time was spent in prolonged visits to relatives, an affliction they felt bound to put up with for sake of family unity. Every year, in late summer or autumn, she came to Aestervoe, staying in alternate years at Grinda Garth and Leabakka.

"You'll likely have a good share of her," Kirsty pointed out. "She'll come over to see you a day now and again, no doubt. The bairns will be back at school by then, that's one mercy."

Charlotte got stiffly to her feet. "I suppose I'd better be making for home. Nina will be wondering what's become of me."

"You'll let us know when you get definite word from Johnny?" Kirsty struggled up and brushed an ant from her apron. "And if I get a hen from Mimie, I'll send the bairns over for the setting of eggs you promised me."

"Fine that. I'll start gathering for you."

They began to move away from each other, homewards, still continuing their conversation. Charlotte crossed the burn and lifted her hand in farewell.

"So, blessing, Kirsty."

"Blessing, lass."

Kirsty started up the slope, hands on her back, and began to sing, "… *and I rise content in the morning …*"

Chapter 9

THE ROAD TO MILBISTER

CARO and Marina were to fetch the broody hen from Milbister. Connie had elected to accompany her grandmother to Leabakka, for the ducklings had just hatched and she was keen to see them. Besides, Milbister was right at the other end of the village and half-way up a hill; it was a long way to walk. Connie wasn't fond of exercise.

Kirsty had prepared the basket with the lid which Joey always used for her shopping, lining it with old newspapers, and Caro and Marina were to take it to put the hen in.

"There's a bit of string inside to tie down the lid, tell Mimie that, and mind you don't open the basket on the way home, or that'll be the last that's seen of Mimie o' Milbister's klokkin hen," Kirsty told them.

They set off, swinging the basket between them. At the bottom of the road, they met Jem Brown, and immediately suggested that she should go with them.

"I'll have to ask Auntie Willa." Jem was not an attractive child to look at; pale-faced, with straggling sandy-coloured hair, and rather prominent light-blue eyes. The girls weren't very fond of Jem. She was altogether too meek and pliable and, perversely, they mistrusted it, but she was one of the family now and they knew, thanks to Kirsty's guidance, that she had to be accepted whatever her faults.

Willa, apparently, gave permission, for soon Jem came running to join them, her brown sandals sending up little bursts of dust from the dry road.

They lingered a while when they came to the road by the sea, for old Hammy Bolt was launching his boat to go fishing, with a great deal of splashing and pushing with the oars, and a considerable amount of very interesting cursing. He managed, at last, to get the boat afloat and the girls proceeded on their way.

Ahead lay the cross-roads, one road going straight up the hill to Milbister, the other branching off and leading to the shop and one or two houses.

Marina stopped so suddenly that Caro, who was holding the other end of the basket, felt the handle being wrenched out of her hand.

"Oh, look! Those Bolt boys! And we've got to go past them."

The Bolt boys were Hammy's grandsons, children of a shiftless family who lived in a dilapidated house along the road. There were six of them altogether, but neither the eldest nor the youngest counted, for the eldest, at fifteen, was far too superior to recognise small girls, and the youngest, aged five, was small enough to be kept in his place. It was the ones in-between who persecuted the younger population of Aestervoe.

And all four were there now. Two were on the beach, throwing stones at the gulls; another was walking slowly along the road, swiping at the grassy verge with a stick; the fourth was whirling an old bicycle-tube round above his head, making a whining sound in the air.

"I'm not going on," Marina said, firmly, beginning to retreat.

Caro seized the basket. "We've got to! We can't go back home without the hen!"

"I'll wait here till you come back, Caro."

"No, we must keep together. We'll just go on quickly and never seem them and maybe they won't bother us," said Caro, knowing that it was a vain hope but imagining Kirsty's wrath if they returned home hen-less.

Marina sniffed, grasped the basket tightly, and followed a step behind Caro. Jem, who still had to make the acquaintance of the Bolt boys, had remained silent, but she went on with them, walking by Caro's side.

The two boys on the road caught sight of them and began to come towards them while, as if by tacit agreement, the other two boys started to walk up the beach. They didn't hurry, and there was something treacherous and malevolent in the very casualness of their approach. They surrounded the girls, four scraggy youngsters, with ragged jerseys, and cruel eyes.

"Where're you going, then?" demanded one.

Caro stuck her chin in the air. "An errand."

"Where to?"

"Milbister."

"What for?"

Caro debated whether to tell him to mind his own business, then decided not to antagonise him, and answered, "A hen."

"Going to eat it? We'll kill it for you."

"It's to set on eggs."

"Well, we'll kill it! When you come back we'll be here and we'll kill it."

Caro tried to push her way between two of the boys but was roughly thrust back again.

"Hey, let's take their shoes and socks and throw them in the sea," suggested one, while the others shrieked their agreement.

There was nothing for it but to fight, out-numbered though they were, and unequal the contest. The boys set about whipping their bare legs, using the stick, the bicycle-tube, and docks pulled from the ditch. Caro struck out with the basket, her only weapon, but Marina was too small and scared to do anything except try to run. It was Jem who battled like a small, flailing fury; she hit out, she kicked, scratched, bit, and pulled their hair.

Then onto the scene came old Mootie Maggie who lived in one tiny, dark room beneath the Hughsons' hay-loft. Mootie Maggie had the reputation, amongst the children, of being a witch. Her appearance now, in her usual rusty black garb, her untidy grey hair flying out in all directions, and calling down all sorts of maledictions, was enough to give credence to the belief. Furthermore, she carried a pair of large, iron tongs which she proceeded to raise in a business-like fashion.

The boys waited for no more; they turned and ran. The girls would have liked to do the same, but there was the basket and one of Marina's sandals to retrieve.

Mootie Maggie turned and hobbled back to her dwelling, still mutterng vindictively under her breath.

"Come on, lets get up the road before the boys come back again," Caro said, breathlessly.

"Is she really a witch?" asked Marina, hurriedly buckling her sandal.

"I don't know, but I'm glad she came. The Bolts were scared, anyway."

At Milbister, they found Mimie singling turnips in the yard behind the house. Caro repeated the message as Kirsty had told her, word for word.

"Please do you have a klokkin hen Mam could get the loan of?"

A smile crossed Mimie's weather-beaten face. "I have three, so she's welcome to one of them. It's an awful job to break them off it, once they start. I've just had to keep throwing them off the nests but I can't be at it all the time. They say if you put them in a basket and hang it on the clothes-line it'll put them off this klokkin, but I have my doubts about that."

She went into the hen-house, bending down to get through the small door. There was an abusive squawking, and Mimie emerged with a Rhode Island Red under her arm, every feather of it standing up separately so that it looked enormous. It seemed quite happy to go into the basket, moving itself into a comfortable position and settling down, clucking to itself.

Mimie regarded it with satisfaction. "It's dead-klokkin, right enough. And the Rhodies always make good klokk's-midders."

As they left the house, they saw four figures away down on the beach. The Bolts were back again.

"I'm not going past *them* again," Marina said. "Let's go round by the main road, Caro."

"Yes, fine," said Caro, no more anxious than Marina to get involved again. Besides, there was the hen to be protected now, as well. To walk round by the main road was over a mile but was preferable to physical assault.

"You fought good, Jem," Caro told her, as they started off along the tarred road which went north.

"I'm used to fighting," Jem said, matter-of-factly. "There were an awful lot of bad boys on Lynna Isle, and some of the girls were almost as bad. There wasn't anybody to stick-up for me, you see. I hadn't any big sisters, and Sydney was only a baby."

Suddenly, Caro had a glimpse of what it would be like to be a solitary child. She, Connie and Marina had their own private disputes but they always stuck together against outside attack.

"Well, you've got us now," she told Jem. "We'll all stand-up for each other."

A shy smile broke over Jem's plain face. She looked pleased, but all she said was, "Yes, OK."

They left the houses behind and there was only the hill on one side, and a moor, running down to a burn, on the other. Occasionally, they glimpsed someone working on a peat-bank, and sometimes they passed a ewe and lamb by the road-side. A car went past, a square, yellow car, with the hood down. It didn't take the turning into Aestervoe but went on and disappeared over the top of the hill.

"See who that was? That Cecil Porter and Miss Isbister!" Caro exclaimed.

"Auntie Willa says all the girls are breaking their necks over Cecil Porter!"

"I heard Ruby Petrie tell Lottie Hoseason that he was some sheik."

"What's a sheik?" asked Jem.

"I don't know. I thought you might," Caro confessed.

"We can ask Joey," Marina suggested, brightly, "she'll know."

They looked at each other and giggled, without quite knowing what they were giggling at.

It took a long time before they reached the Grinda Garth road. Caro and Marina parted from Jem, who said, reluctantly, that she had best go straight home. The other two struggled on up the road, their arms aching from carrying the basket, for although the hen wasn't as heavy as its fluffed-out appearance had suggested, it had taken them such a long time to get home.

Kirsty was standing at the gate, looking for them. "Bairns, I was beginning to wonder what had happened to you."

"Are you going to set the hen right now?" demanded Marina. "Can we come and watch?"

"No, no, my bairn. I've made ready a box of hay with a china nest-egg in it and we'll put her there and see if she is going to sit. If she settles down, we'll put the eggs under her tomorrow."

It was dim and musty in the barn where Kirsty had put the box. There was a little gap between the stones, at one end, where a ray from the setting sun shone in, and dust-motes wavered in the yellow light. All the crofting implements were kept here; the spades, forks, hoes, the tuskars for peat-cutting, and the horse-harness.

In a corner, there was a rough, wooden structure where the potatoes were kept, and various baskets and kishies hung round the walls. The children didn't like the barn much; they felt that the stone crevices contained spiders, and similar evils, only waiting to pounce.

Mimie's hen settled down quite well, ruffling its feathers, and using its beak to push the china egg in between its large and ugly feet. It then sat down with a little wriggling movement of its body. Kirsty covered over half of the top of the box with a piece of cardboard and they left the barn, carefully closing the door.

"What about her supper?" asked Caro.

"Oh, we'll give her something in the morning. A klokkin hen eats very little, you know."

Connie was sitting on the doorstep, eating a piece of raw rhubarb. "Johnny is coming home next week," she greeted them. "Auntie Charlotte is sewing a new quilt for his room. It's got all different kinds of material in it. And Uncle Gibbie is distempering the porch a sort of green colour. Auntie Charlotte says she hopes it'll be alright, for green is unlucky, but it was the only colour left in the shop. She wanted Sunshine Yellow."

Caro scraped at the lichen on the wall, with her finger. "What was Nina doing?"

"She'd gone over to Timmy Gray's with the wireless accumulator. He charges it up on his engine."

"I wish we had a wireless," sighed Caro.

"Arthur's saving up for one. He said so."

"It's taking him an awful long time. I don't think he gets much money at the shop."

"He spends a lot on clothes. I heard Mam asking him when he was getting his spats."

"What's spats?"

"I don't know. He was mad."

Connie got up. The stone doorstep was chilly through her pink cotton frock. The sun had set now, away in the north-west, and the voe was calm, with the dusky hills beyond. In the long grass, beyond the yard fence, Tammas was stalking moths which hovered and spun on silvery wings. He would make sudden, wild lunges in mid-air, waving his paws.

Caro realised that she felt cold now, and turned to go into the house. "Arthur is so silly, sometimes," she remarked.

"Sometimes," said Connie, "I wish Johnny lived with us, instead of Arthur."

"If he did, we'd have a wireless by now!" Caro answered.

Chapter 10

SUMMER SUNDAY

IF JOEY was disappointed that the wedding had been postponed, she gave no sign of it. Outwardly, she was just the same even-tempered Joey she had always been. Even to herself, she made no attempt to analyse her feelings on the matter, except that she admitted she was just as well pleased that she hadn't bought her wedding clothes after all.

She wondered how May and Belle would feel. They had had their dresses for all of three months. She had not seen much of Hugh's sisters lately. Once, she had called at Gardie Hill, after an evening service in the Wastervoe church and, afterwards, May and Belle had walked part of the way home with her.

She had invited them to come to Grinda Garth some Sunday, to spend the afternoon and stay to tea. But she had been surprised when they had actually done so. It had not been a great success.

Tom had gone to Lynna Isle to see to the disposal of his cousin's effects, Willa was in bed with a bad cold, and she had sent the children to Grinda Garth for the day. Jem was amenable enough but two-year-old Sydney was proving to be a handful. He had screamed with bad-temper for most of the time and, at tea, had deliberately upset the milk-jug and had kicked everyone within range of his short, fat legs.

In the melee, Kirsty had tripped over Tammas while carrying the teapot and had scalded her hand. May and Belle, stiff at the best of times, had made no attempt to smooth things over, or to hide their annoyance, and had left as soon as the tea was over, even before Joey had begun to clear away the dishes.

After they had gone, Joey felt a vague restlessness. She had planned to accompany them a little way along the road to Wastervoe, expecting their departure to be rather later, about the time, perhaps, when Nina and the other girls would be on their way back from their Sunday evening walk, and she could have joined up with them and had a little of their cheerful company. Sunday evenings could be dull, with Hugh away, and nothing much to do.

It was a beautiful evening. After a breezy, sunny day, the wind had dropped and the voe was a pale turquoise with dark, calm patches round the shore. Joey wasn't conscious that she sighed as she sat down in the restin-shair and picked up the latest *John Bull*.

Kirsty, her hand bandaged, and seeming none the worse of her injury, was laboriously writing to a cousin in Leith. She looked up, and said, "Is there no' a meeting in the mission hall tonight? I thought I heard someone mention it …"

"I believe there is," Joey replied, "at seven, if I mind right."

"Why don't you take the bairns and go?"

Joey considered. It wasn't a bad idea. There was no church in Aestervoe, but she often attended the meetings in the non-denominational Mission Hall, down by the shore.

The children, who were amusing themselves out-of-doors in a desultory Sunday fashion, were called in to be tidied and dressed in their best coats and the cream, straw hats trimmed with rosebuds and ribbons. Connie, who wasn't fashion-conscious, preferring comfort to elegance, objected to wearing her new patent-leather shoes and didn't see why her sandals couldn't do, if they were polished-up, but she was over-ruled, as she had known she would be.

Joey surveyed them; Connie in blue, Caro in apple-green, and Marina in rose-pink, and was satisfied that no part of their toilet had been neglected. She turned to Jem, who had been allowed to stay and play at Grinda Garth, though Sydney had been returned home. Jem was wearing a tan-coloured coat which did nothing for her sallow skin, and a yellow beret, which was even worse.

Something would have to be done for the child, Joey reflected. But what? Willa wouldn't take kindly to advice. Meantime, she pulled the beret off Jem's head and, going upstairs, returned with Marina's last summer's straw hat. It was too small to sit properly on Marina's thick locks, but would fit over Jem's fine, thin hair. The hat was a little faded in places but was an improvement on the awful yellowness of the beret.

"Now, here are your pennies for the collection. Don't lose them."

"You'd better keep a hold of the collections and give them to the bairns when they come round with the box, Joey," advised Kirsty. "Otherwise, they are sure to drop the pennies on the floor and make a disturbance."

The Mission Hall was a tiny place with a bare wooden floor and hard, varnished benches. At the far end there was a space, with benches for the choir, the harmonium, and, in the centre, the pulpit, an ugly, clumsy structure varnished dark-brown.

Each week there was a different preacher and tonight it was the turn of the Wesleyan minister from Sandayre, a scraggy little man, middle-aged, with a reddish nose, and puckish, twinkling eyes.

Joey shepherded the children into a seat near the back and alongside one of the windows which overlooked the road and the beach. They were early, so they had a chance to view everyone as they came in, a pastime which, for Caro, was the highlight of the whole meeting.

John Petrie, the shopkeeper, arrived with his thin, little wife whose boiled-gooseberry eyes looked ready to pop out on stalks. John Petrie looked very dignified in striped trousers and a gold watch-chain straddling his fat stomach. The five Hoseason sisters, from Houll, came next, the three eldest taking their places on the choir-benches. They were all quite different in appearance: Cissie, the eldest, was short and fat; Janet, tall and hefty; Barbara Ann was tall and thin; Lottie was short and thin; while Alexina was average in both directions.

Nina smiled across at Joey and the children as she went into the choir. Auntie Charlotte and Uncle Gibbie chose a seat across the passage-way. Auntie Charlotte was wearing a felt hat with a brim and a large bow of gathered ribbon. Uncle Gibbie had on small, very shiny boots which creaked as he walked.

Lizzie Spence, who kept lodgers, came and sat in front of the Mouats, and Marina glared at the large expanse of back in the tight brown coat which obscured her view, while Connie wrinkled her nose in disgust at the powerful aroma of mothballs.

Mootie Maggie slipped, like a shadow, into a back seat, her hair twisted into an untidy bun below a black hat, green with age. Caro turned her head to peer at her. Joey nudged her, and Caro wriggled, but turned back obediently. The minister was arriving and, behind him, Mina Coutts, who played the harmonium.

There were two hymns and a prayer to begin with, and then the congregation settled down to listen to the sermon. In the choir space, someone was passing round peppermints, and there was some shuffling and coughing as everyone made themselves comfortable. It was warm in the small building, with the evening sun shining in through the windows and making bright squares on the cream-painted walls.

The children had little interest in the sermon and their eyes began to look for some more entertaining way to fill the time. Marina started to take an interest in a large blue-bottle, as it crawled up the window-pane, then dropped to the sill, then continued its pointless excursion up the pane again. Connie was flicking over the pages of her hymn-book, in its soft, bright-blue covers. Caro was covertly looking out of the window, watching the wild Bolt boys throwing stones at the boats which were moored off-shore. Only Jem sat with eyes turned towards the pulpit, mouth slightly open, as if mentally digesting every word.

A lethargic drowsiness seemed to pervade the congregation, with the exception of John Petrie, who grunted, nodded, moaned, or shook his head, as the sermon proceeded. Then the preacher was announcing the last hymn. Everyone bestirred themselves with sighs and near-yawns and creaking of the wooden benches. The harmonium wheezed into life, and they all stood up to sing *Wonderful Words of Life*.

Outside, a few words of conversation were exchanged and then began the leisurely walk homewards. All around lay the peacefulness of a summer Sunday evening. The steep road up from the shore was fringed with cow-parsley and wild iris, with dandelions, daisies, and buttercups at their roots and, in the field beyond, the hay had been mown and put up, beige-coloured domes on greenish patches.

Soon after Joey and the girls turned onto the main road, they came to the house of Hivdalea, with its bare, uncurtained windows and air of desertion. Caro pointed to it, importantly, and said to Jem, "That's where Joey is going to live when she gets married. Isn't it, Joey?"

"Yes, dear."

"Couldn't we go up and look at it?"

Why not? Joey only hesitated for a moment, then slipped the catch from the gate and pushed it open. Closely followed by the children, she went up the narrow path, thrusting aside the tangled branches of the gooseberry bushes. Something would have to be done to prevent them encroaching further over the path. And the steps at the tumble-down porch were full of cracks, and wasn't that chimney-pot at a peculiar angle?

The girls were peering in at the windows, cupping their hands at the sides of their faces to block the light. Marina swung round, holding up one foot and hopping on the other.

"Can we go inside, Joey?"

Joey shook her head. "There's no way of getting in."

If only Hugh had left the key with her, she could have come down in her spare time, tidied up a bit, or at least put fires on to help air the place. But – he hadn't. Presumably, he would have left the key at home. Perhaps, next time she was at Gardie Hill, she could ask about it.

"It doesn't look very clean," Connie said, fastidiously, "and the wallpaper is hanging down in strips."

"It'll need a lot done to it. It's been totally neglected since the Hunters left," Joey sighed.

She stepped back and glanced at the upstairs windows where, at one of them, hung the tattered remains of a lace half-curtain. It looked worse, even, than the bare windows, lending a desolate, forsaken atmosphere to the house.

She turned quickly and went back down the path to the gate, the children trailing reluctantly behind. As she closed the gate, she couldn't help looking back at the house again. It was just an untenanted building; she felt no sense of belonging to it, or it to her.

That night, she went to bed and dreamed that the garden of Hivdalea was bright with yellow flowers. When she woke, she recalled the meaning of dream-colours – red for scandal, purple for a space of time, yellow for forsaken …

Chapter 11

JOHNNY COMES MARCHING HOME

JOHNNY came home on a rainy August day with a near-gale blowing from the south, and the voe and sky and distant hills lost in a dreary grey. Kirsty watched from the porch window for his arrival, and saw him crossing the grass between the road and Leabakka, his canvas sailor's-bag on his shoulder, while his father walked beside him, carrying his suitcase. Nina left the house and went to meet them, while Charlotte hovered at the gate in the shelter of the house wall.

"He's come!" Kirsty announced, with satisfaction.

That evening, Johnny came over to Grinda Garth, together with Charlotte and Nina.

"Auntie Kirsty!" he embraced her vigorously then held her at arm's length "as good looking as ever!"

"Och, Johnny," Kirsty tittered, "you and your nonsense."

Johnny had his father's build; not more than average in height, slim and agile, with straight, silky blond hair, and blue eyes in a face that had somehow become tanned in spite of a fair complexion. He kissed Joey, swung the children off their feet, shook hands with Magnie and Davie and slapped Arthur on the back. Buoyant, debonair, cheerful – that was Johnny.

Even Arthur had taken the night off from pursuing his stagnant love-affair to welcome Johnny home again. The two had always been great friends although Johnny was Arthur's senior by three years, and much more in experience and judgement.

Johnny had brought presents for the children and the womenfolk, and as each was produced Kirsty exclaimed over it with surprise, though she would have been more surprised had there been none. For the girls there were tartan, pleated skirts, for Joey, silk kimono pyjamas and, for Kirsty, two framed, Japanese prints of flowers and birds.

They settled down by the fire, while the rain trickled down the window, and the outside door, which had shrunk during the dry spell, rattled loosely with every gust of wind. Johnny had to hear all the island news. About how the new steamer wasn't coming this summer, after all; and how, when Nettie Blance had married Ertie Simpson, she had said that she couldn't invite those who had been her old boyfriends for Ertie would be jealous.

Johnny fingered his chin and looked solemn. "That could have caused complications."

"It did that. They say Lizzie Charleson never spoke to her man for two months, for they weren't asked to the wedding and Nettie her second cousin."

And there was the story of the new minister over at Burrawick who had turned up late for a christening because he had fallen in a midden and had to return home to be cleaned up.

"He'd had more than a drink of water before leaving the manse, I'll be bound," said Kirsty, slanderously, giving a tug at her ball of wool which sent it rolling underneath the restin-shair where Gaerd slept uncomfortably with his head on one of Magnie's wooden-soled clogs.

Marina went to retrieve it, and Johnny winked at her as she passed his chair. "And what have you lasses been up to while I've been away?" he asked. "Have you got yourself a man yet, Marina?"

Marina, looking scandalised, shook her head. "We've got a new teacher," she volunteered.

"A new teacher, eh? Well, that's the next best thing. Is she young? And pretty?"

Marina considered, "Yes, she's sort of young. She's got red hair."

"Well, well! I'll need to try my luck there. With a red-haired teacher for a wife a chap could retire and put his feet on the mantelpiece."

Marina laughed, and the gap in her teeth showed comically. "She goes for drives with Cecil Porter."

Johnny pretended to glower. "Oho, who is this Cecil Porter who thinks he can do me out of a red-haired wife?"

Arthur, looking rather fiery in the face, said, "Oh, can't you be quiet for two minutes, Marina?"

Which Marina thought rather unfair, seeing she had been having a sensible conversation with Johnny.

Johnny glanced at Arthur and drew his own conclusions. He gave Marina's cardigan a tweak and said, "Oh, I think I'll just wait for you to grow-up, after all. Better the devil you know than the devil you don't."

Charlotte looked across at him over the top of her knitting, pursing her mouth and shaking her head. "Johnny, Johnny! What a thing to say in front of the bairns!"

There wasn't much force behind her rebuke and Johnny only laughed. "Is it true the regatta is next week?" he asked. "I'm glad I'm home in time for that."

As the conversation turned to future social events, Joey began to feel a little uncomfortable. She had, in fact, looked forward to Johnny's arrival with mixed feelings. She had hinted pretty strongly that she was going to ask Johnny to be best-man at the wedding, and now there wasn't going to be a wedding; at least, not this year. Supposing he asked about her forthcoming marriage? He might even tease her about it – Johnny was a great one for teasing.

But he didn't. She realised that Johnny wouldn't say anything to cause her embarrassment; she ought to have known that. Perhaps he might mention it if they were alone. Johnny had all his mother's shrewdness, allied to an unusual delicacy of feeling. She rose to make the eight o'clock's tea, feeling easier in her mind now.

Davie had set up an iron-last on a chair by the window, preparatory to mending a pair of shoes. He said, "Are you home for long, Johnny?"

"Oh, he'll surely stay a while, now he's come," Charlotte said, hopefully.

Johnny looked thoughtful. "I haven't made up my mind, definitely. But I've a kind of fancy to have Christmas at home. It's seven years since I last did."

A slow smile spread over Charlotte's homely countenance, but her fingers remained busy with her knitting.

When the tea was over, Johnny announced that he would have to "Take a run down and see Willa," and suggested that Nina and Joey should go with him. Nina declined. She wasn't over-fond of Willa, but excused herself by saying that she wanted to get on with the jumper she was knitting, which was true enough, anyway.

"Well, you'll come, Joey? Or do you mind the rain?"

Joey laughed. "I'll come! Just wait till I find my rubber boots."

"I hear," said Johnny, as they went down the road, "that Willa and Tom have a ready-made family."

"Yes," said Joey, "at least, for the time being, but we don't know if it's to be a permanent arrangement."

Willa had given the impression that she would be happy to adopt Sydney, but Jem was a different proposition. It was unlikely, however, that Tom would agree to parting the small brother and sister, and he treated both children the same. Poor, unloved little Jem! She was so amenable, so desperately anxious to please, yet her very docility seemed to arouse impatience, if not antagonism, in Willa. Perhaps, if Jem had been a pretty child … However, she wasn't, and her diffident nature, added to a wishy-washy appearance, made her simply a shadow.

Willa's home was a cheerless dwelling. A meagre fire smouldered feebly in the small black stove which hadn't been black-leaded for days, to judge by the look of it. The floor was unswept, and a pile of dirty dishes overflowed from a basin on the table. Willa was sitting in a chair by the stove, rocking a red-faced and glowering Sydney on her lap, but she seemed genuinely pleased to see Johnny.

"It's a pity Tom is out. Bobby Spence had to go over to Sandvoe with his cow and he sent word to see if Tom could go with him. It'll likely be midnight before they get back." She hugged Sydney closer to her, adding, "And this little man isn't well. It's his teeth, I think."

Joey looked at the round, sullen face under the mop of almost-white curls, and thought that 'his temper' would have been a more accurate diagnosis. Kirsty, who had at first thought that having two children to look after could only do Willa good, had changed her opinion. She had noted Willa's obsession with the boy, had summed up the calculating look in the wide blue eyes of Sydney, and had remarked to herself, "Sly. There'll be trouble there, later on, I'll be bound."

Willa turned sharply to Jem who had pressed herself into the furthest corner of the couch as if trying to become invisible. "Fetch some peats for the fire. The bucket's empty."

Jem immediately slid down from the couch and reached for the bucket, but Joey forestalled her. "I'll go, Jem."

However, Jem followed her out into the porch and waited while she filled the bucket from the peat-bunker, and when they returned to the living-room Johnny was unpacking the box he had brought with him.

Willa exclaimed over the lace tablecloth, and then Johnny handed her some money. "I didn't know what to get for your family," he said, "not being sure of their ages. Buy something for the boy, from me."

His eyes met Joey's and, perhaps recognising the appeal in them, and also having realised that Sydney was very much Willa's favourite, he passed a note to her. "And Joey can get something for – Jem, isn't it – as she's well used to small girls!"

Willa made no objection. She probably would have done had Joey offered to take the money and buy for Jem, but it had been Johnny's suggestion, and her interest in the girl was so slight that she didn't mind being relieved of what would only have been a chore. She certainly didn't recognise that Johnny had a motive for bringing Joey into it.

The wind had backed easterly when Joey and Johnny started back for Grinda Garth, and the sea was washing against the Wastervoe shore in white ruffles. In the north-by field, the lambs lay in the shelter of their mothers, and Peggie and Pride turned their backs to the wind and went on cropping the lush grass which had been made fresher and greener by the rain.

Joey tentatively broached the question she had been wanting to ask. "I don't suppose you saw anything of Hugh while you were away?"

"I met in with him a couple of times," Johnny answered, but didn't enlarge on the topic.

Joey was uneasily aware of some unaccountable restraint in him. She wondered if he, like Kirsty, had formed a dislike for Hugh; but that wasn't characteristic of Johnny who was hail-fellow-well-met with everyone.

Johnny, seeming to become aware of the constrained atmosphere between them, said, "I don't know him at all well, you know. We've never been shipmates, but I've seen him once or twice in the Sailors' Home. He's just left on another trip, hasn't he?"

"Yes," said Joey, and left it at that. There didn't seem to be anything more to say. But she couldn't rid herself of the feeling that Johnny could have said more, had he wished.

Chapter 12

THE REGATTA

THE Wastervoe regatta took place in the last week of the school holidays and was spread over two days. The evening before day one, a motor-boat toured through the voe laying buoys to mark the course. The children found this exciting, the forerunner of the entertainment to come, and ran to the beach to watch the mooring of the buoy which lay just off the Aestervoe shore, coming back with sandals soaked with sea-water.

On the first day, the second-class boats raced, first sailing the length of the voe and then out into the firth. Each time the boats appeared at the entrance to the voe, the girls set off to the shore to watch them round the buoy. It was part of the whole enjoyment, running with the cloud-shadows against a lilting south wind. When old Hammy Bolt, steering his somewhat dilapidated boat *The Flower of the Isles*, had his cap blown off by a gust of wind, the girls felt that they had extracted the last ounce of merriment from the day.

On the second day, in addition to the day's racing of the first-class boats, there were rowing races and a programme of land-sports at Wastervoe. By eight-thirty, the boats lying at the Wastervoe pier were getting their sails up. Both Davie and Johnny were participating as crew members and the girls were torn between 'sticking up' for Daddy's boat, or for Johnny's, and thinking it would be fair if both should win a race.

About eleven o'clock, Joey, Magnie, Arthur, and the girls, set out for the beach from where they would take the rowing-boat across to Wastervoe. Kirsty, whose interest in the proceedings was negligible, was staying at home to "see to things," and perhaps would have a run over to Leabakka during the afternoon, for Charlotte, too, would be staying behind.

Joey, carrying the girls' coats in case it became cooler later on, came last in the small procession. She walked carefully in her first-time-on beige sandals. It was a perfect morning. The track ran down alongside cultivated fields, potatoes, turnips, and grain, and on the other side there were long, green reeds which tickled the bare legs and arms of the children as they brushed past.

At the entrance to the voe, the headland sat flatly on the pale water, like a pointed, dark cap, and round its rim the white cotton-plant lay like drifts of snow.

Magnie and Arthur held the boat steady while the others clambered in. Arthur was in great good humour. He was certain that he and a friend would win the two-man pulling race, and surely that would make Babs Isbister sit up and take notice! He could talk of little else but the race and the technique they meant to employ.

Magnie said, "Hmph!" but made no other comment. He gave the impression of having little confidence in Arthur's ability to win a rowing race.

There was a sizeable crowd of spectators on the pier, all in holiday mood. The girls gazed with admiration at the flags which fluttered from the poles along the pier, and at the lines of colourful pennants strung between the buildings. Unused to crowds, they kept very close to Joey who was wandering about rather aimlessly, chatting to people she knew. Except for the sailing, there wasn't much to see at present as the other events wouldn't take place until the afternoon.

Just after one o'clock, they went to the church-hall which was being utilised as a tea-room. Women from both sides of the voe were acting as cooks, waitresses, and washers-up, wearing their best aprons over 'good' dresses.

At the far end of the room, pots of water were being boiled on the small stove and, whenever anyone lifted a lid, a white cloud of steam rose upwards towards the discoloured ceiling. Little trickles of moisture ran down the painted wooden walls, and there was a hot, humid atmosphere which caught one's breath.

Nina was doing a shift in the tea-room. She saw Joey and the girls and came over with their tea in thick, white cups, and a paper-bag for each of them, containing a butter sandwich, a German bun, and two plain, sweet biscuits.

"It's been a hectic morning," said Nina, pushing back a strand of hair from her hot face. "The fine day has brought out the crowd, just like the fishy-bees! I've only got another hour to do, though."

"That's good, you'll be able to watch the sports with us," said Joey.

"Yes, and I'd love to enter the three-legged race. Joey, would you come with me?"

Joey laughed. She didn't share Nina's zeal for participation. There was too much reserve in her nature. Sometimes, she suspected that she missed out on a lot of fun because of it. She hesitated then gave Nina a half-promise.

An elderly woman in a black, marocain dress, a string of amber beads, and with a budding moustache, bustled up to the table and told Nina to collect the used crockery from a table which had just been vacated. She appeared to consider herself to be in charge. Nina gave Joey a rueful look, and went.

When they left the tea-room, the sports were getting underway in a nearby field. The girls, who were beginning to feel more at ease now, didn't need much encouragement from

Joey to enter the children's competitions. Nina joined them in time for the senior fun-and-games and she and Joey succeeded in coming second in the three-legged race, but Joey could not be prevailed upon to enter for the sack-race. Nina took part, however, and distinguished herself by falling in a cow-pat.

"That's one of the reasons why I wouldn't enter," Joey told her. "I saw a cow tethered over there yesterday when I was watching the sailing through the binoculars."

"Oh well, the sack got most of the damage," Nina said, philosophically, scrubbing at the sleeve of her frock with a handful of grass.

They walked down to the pier to watch the rowing-races. Cecil Porter's car went trundling past with much rattling of loose mudguards and running-boards. Babs Isbister was sitting beside him.

Nina laughed. "There goes the Sheik of Araby! One of these days that car is going to fall to pieces on the road around him."

"That's Miss Isbister!" said Marina.

"Yes, dear," said Nina, and added, "that won't go down well in some quarters!"

Joey shook her head, and smiled, "She's a hard-sought woman, as Auntie Kirsty would say. I wonder who will finally win the day?"

"The highest bidder, I should think!"

"Oh, Nina!" Joey was half-shocked, half-amused.

By four-thirty, people were beginning to make their way homewards, for there was the concert and dance to get ready for. The party from Grinda Garth, which now included Davie, who had finished with the day's sailing, cautiously descended the slippery steps at the side of the pier and got into the boat.

Arthur's good spirits of the morning hadn't survived the two-man pulling-race, during which he had first lost his oar, then toppled backwards over the seat into the bottom of the boat. The laughter of the spectators still echoed in his ears. He was convinced he would hear it until his dying day. Consequently, he was in a captious mood, snapping at the children, and irritated by the slow, deliberate movements of his father.

A little way ahead, the Leabakka boat headed for the shore, with Johnny rowing. Nina was sitting in the stern, trailing her fingers in the water. The wind had fallen away to nothing and the air had a slight heaviness about it. Later on, probably, midges would arise in swarms.

The dark water chopped against the boat and, in spite of Arthur's set, morose face, Joey was aware of the kind of tranquillity that one only finds on the sea.

The keel of the boat grated on the stony beach, and Caro intensified her hints about wanting to go to the concert. Joey hadn't planned to go and Davie would be too tired after two days of sailing to want to row across to Wastervoe, and back again, tonight. And with Arthur in so sullen a mood, he certainly would not be offering to give the children a night out. Joey sighed. She hoped Caro wasn't going to be awkward.

However, during tea, Kirsty announced that the chickens were due to hatch the following day, and that she was going to listen to the eggs that night to see if she could hear any movement, and Caro's interest immediately became centred on this forthcoming event.

"You haven't seen anything of Willa, I suppose?" Joey asked.

She knew that Willa had intended to take the children to the regatta. Tom had hired one of the three taxis in Wastervoe to fetch them, but there had been no sign of them all day.

"Och!" Kirsty put down her cup with a rattle which expressed her exasperation. "I saw Jem playing in the back-green so I went down to see why they hadn't gone to the regatta and then Willa is sitting in front of a fire that could have roasted an ox, with the boy on her lap, and saying he's got a fever and she couldn't take him out. If I had stayed in that kippering-kiln ten minutes longer I'd have had a fever myself!"

"I wish I'd taken Jem with us," said Joey.

"Never speak! It must have been disappointing for the bairn, not that she would ever have said anything, poor infant."

After tea, Arthur had to be got ready for the concert and dance. Kirsty had ironed the wrong shirt, he declared. Joey, rummaging amongst the clean clothes in the cupboard, was thankful to find that the shirt he wanted had, at least, been washed. Kirsty drew hot coals from the fire out onto the hearthstone and set the irons to heat. Caro and Marina were commanded to search under the restin-shair for his shoes, and Davie, forestalling his mother, said he would brush them.

"I put a pair of clean socks on your bed," Kirsty told Arthur. "It's a pair Magnie made on the sock-machine last winter, and maybe they are on the thick side, but your cashmere ones had holes in both heels."

"I've got a pair of silk socks," said Arthur, trying to be matter-of-fact, and sounding self-conscious.

"Silk socks! It'll be spats next," said his mother.

"They were selling them off at the shop. I got them cheap," said Arthur, defensively.

"Then they'll likely have moths in them. Nobody ever got a bargain out of John Petrie yet. He's got gripping-sense, that one."

Arthur set off at last, in his blue serge suit and white shirt, his light-blue tie almost – but not quite – matching the pale-blue silk socks. Joey felt as if a whirlwind had passed through the house. She went into the porch and measured out the corn for the hens from the sack in one of the cupboards. It was early for their last feed, but she felt in need of a breath of air and a chance to be on her own, even for five minutes.

The August evening was still and sunny. The voe black-shadowed, with long, slow ripples, and pastel reflections from the lemon-coloured north-west sky. The firth was as clear and colourless as a mirror. Across the burn, Nina was making for the road where three of the Hoseason girls were waiting. She was carefully holding up her long, blue evening-dress at one side.

Joey turned away and went on towards the hen-house. The hens, recognising their feeding-basin, flocked to meet her, running like stout, clumsy matrons, with wings half-spread. Tomorrow was a mail-day, Joey thought. Perhaps she would have a letter from Hugh.

Nina came over next day, ostensibly to borrow a jumper-board, but bursting to impart all the news of the dance. Joey walked down to the burn with her.

"… and Janet was there, sporting her engagement ring! She's caught Sammy Irvine at last – and I don't think it'll be long to the wedding by what Alexina was saying. You know, Joey, it's terrible, everyone's dropping-out – the old gang, I mean. First you, now Janet …"

"I haven't gone yet," said Joey, and wondered what had made her say that.

"No, but – and just imagine, Johnny went off with Netta Burgoyne! I was teasing him this morning about it and he said she was the only girl left on her own at the end of the dance so there was nothing else for it! But I saw them together long before that time."

"Netta's a very pleasant girl, though she never has much to say."

"But she's such a dumpling! It doesn't matter what she wears she always succeeds in looking like a sack of meal tied round the middle. And she's got a bit of a squint."

"It doesn't show so much now she's got glasses."

Nina laughed. "I know. I'm being nasty. It's just that I'd never have guessed she'd be Johnny's type – or anybody's, come to that – and there I go again!"

"Well, everyone to his taste, as the man said when he kissed the cow! Tell me, Nina, did you see anything of Babs Isbister ... and Arthur?"

Nina wrinkled her brow. "Oh, she was dancing with Cecil Porter the whole night. I can't understand what she sees in him. If you really look him over he seems just ordinary and rather gawky. I thought he wasn't bad, at first, but I think it was just the glamour of the car! I believe that's why she keeps hanging on to him, just so she can be transported everywhere and be a cut above the rest of us."

It appeared that Arthur shared this opinion. As Joey was setting the tea, an extraordinary racket cut through the quiet of the late afternoon; distant, at first, but gradually becoming more persistent until it seemed to fill the air. Joey went out to the porch door. Kirsty had stopped on the step on her way in from the rain-tub with a bucket of water to boil the hens' potatoes. She was looking towards the road, shading her eyes with her hand.

Joey turned her head in the same direction in time to see the motor-cyclist come into view, wobbling precariously up the rough, stony road. The cacophony of sound became more pronounced, a strident mixture of engine noise and body vibration.

The motor-cycle came to a halt, rather too abruptly, at the gate, almost precipitating the rider over the handlebars. There was considerable spluttering and popping before the engine was shut off and Arthur said, unnecessarily, "I've bought a motor-bike."

"The Good Man preserve us!" said Kirsty.

Caro, peeping from the safety of the byre gable, thought indignantly, "He's spent the wireless money on a bike!"

Chapter 13

THE BERRY-HILL

ARTHUR had bought the second-hand Douglas in the hope of appearing more desirable in the eyes of Babs Isbister but his obsession with the motor-cycle itself almost superseded the first ambition. He spent endless hours cleaning and oiling, adjusting chains, mending punctures – all of it quite unnecessary, according to Kirsty who declared that it made no difference what he did, it sounded just the same as it had always done.

Arthur, in his infatuation, was showing more patience than he had ever done before, and would painstakingly try to explain just what he had done to the engine, and what the results had been, but Kirsty would have none of it.

"Why can't you leave it alone as long as it keeps going, instead of forever purling in it? It surely must be a good bike to stand up to the treatment it gets from you," she would proclaim.

The motor-cycle was yet another time-waster, in Kirsty's eyes. They had got one hay-dess in the yard, but there would be another, and meanwhile it was still standing on the rigs; and soon it would be time to cut the corn; then the peats had to be carted home, a job which had to be fitted in between the work of attending to the crops, and the year was spending. Kirsty began to get flustered.

Arthur's preoccupation was bad enough, but when Davie, incredibly, began to show an interest in the motor-cycle – even going so far as to buy a side-car to fit to it – Kirsty's agitation became more pronounced.

"They're worse than two bairns," she declared to Joey, with a sweeping gesture of her hand which landed smartly on the haunches of Tammas and knocked him off the arm of the restins-hair. He took himself off to the comparative safety of the hearthstone where he indulged in an angry frenzy of washing.

"And what need I speak?" Kirsty went on. "It's like water on a duck's back! I may as well hold my tongue."

But she didn't. Instead, she went out to the end of the byre where Arthur and Davie were leaning over the upturned bike and looking as anxious as inexperienced parents regarding their first-born.

Joey watched in rueful amusement from the window. She saw Kirsty point to where Magnie was rebuilding the hay, taken down that morning to dry in the fresh southerly breeze. Davie pulled a tuft of grass and rubbed it over his hands, then made his way down over the rig, with the same slow, deliberate gait as his father. He looked rather like a chastened schoolboy.

Arthur, however, continued to slowly turn one of the wheels and peer into the works of the machine.

Kirsty came back into the house. "That's one of them set on, anyway," she announced with some satisfaction.

The motor-cycle did prove beneficial in some ways, for Arthur was always willing to run errands or to drive anyone anywhere. On one wet and windy Wednesday afternoon, his half-day off from the store, he even collected the children from school on his own initiative. The children began to regard Arthur with more respect. They begged lifts with unwonted humility, and Arthur granted their requests with much outward show of doing them a favour. Secretly, he would have been very disappointed if they had shown no interest. He liked to show-off to an audience, even if it was only six-year-old Marina.

One August Sunday, while Grinda Garth drowsed in the afternoon sun, and Magnie and Tammas kept each other company in the living-room, the only sounds that of the rustle of Magnie's newspaper and the slow, methodical ticking of the American clock on the mantelpiece, Joey and Kirsty were outside viewing the chicks.

The sun was hot on Joey's bare arms. She had put on the new frock which she had bought at the beginning of the summer. It had cost seven-and-sixpence and she had intended to keep it for her trousseau but, somehow, she had wanted to wear it that day and, after all, once wouldn't harm it ... It was a beige colour, with a frill round the Peter Pan collar and down the front of the bodice, edged in green, and with cuffed half-sleeves with the same green edging. Kirsty, too, was wearing her Sunday best, black, with a design in white and grey. She even wore a string of Venetian glass beads and a 'Mizpah' brooch.

The chicks were three weeks old now. They scurried after their mother with little darts and bobs, with occasional deviations off-course to investigate something real or imaginary in the grass. The big Rhode Island Red plodded along, stopping every few steps to scratch the ground with ugly, carbuncled feet, often sending one of her unwary offspring flying out behind. She clucked incessantly, and looked huge, with her fluffed-out pens, yet weighed as light, literally, as a bundle of feathers.

"What do you think, Joey? Are we going to have more hens than cocks?"

Joey shook her head. "It's too soon to tell."

Kirsty looked at the chicks with skilled eyes and pointed to a small, round, black one. "That's a hen, or I'm a Dutchman. But that white one – and the one next to it – both cocks! Their tail-pens are growing already."

"Do you not think that's just the look of the Leghorn? They're spare, bony-looking birds ..."

"Maybe. I hope so. But on my reckoning there's at least seven cocks among them. Still, they'll maybe alter out of it."

Gaerd's black-and-white face appeared round the corner of the barn and he began to pad along the brigstanes towards them. The big Rhodie lifted her head, gave a warning squawk, and made a short run at him, neck stretched, yellow-rimmed eyes bright with the light of battle. Gaerd retired apologetically.

"She's made a fine klokk's-midder," commented Kirsty, as she turned towards the house. "Well, likely time to see to the tea. I wonder where everybody is?"

"The girls went for a walk along the burn – Jem is with them – and Davie went down to speak to Tom, something about mending the cart-road ..."

"Something to be discussing on the Sabbath day!" muttered Kirsty, disapprovingly.

"... and Arthur ..."

"Och, Arthur! The whole world knows where he is, for they hear him that never see him."

As if in answer to a cue, the clamour of the motor-cycle coming up the road reached their ears, and Arthur appeared over the top of the slope, a flurry of light-brown dust rising from his back-wheel. It seemed only seconds until he was running up the path to the door, leaving the motor-cycle propped against the gate-post, and bursting into the living-room behind his mother and Joey.

"Do you know what Alec Coutts is telling me? That Faroese man who is sailing alone from Iceland is due in Lerwick any day now, and they think he'll be passing north by here tonight. Some ship had spotted him and radioed."

"Poor soul, he'll be glad it's a fine night," Kirsty remarked.

"I'm going north a bit to see if I can catch a glimpse of him. Where's Davie? He'll maybe want to come, too."

"You'll have your tea first," Kirsty said, firmly, "and I see Davie crossing the green now."

Arthur was reluctant to wait, but Davie, who had heard the rumour from Tom, assured him that there was no particular hurry. Nevertheless, Arthur sat edgily all through tea – "Like a cat on hot coals," Kirsty said – and was pacing the floor long before Davie, who was deliberately buttering a slice of home-baked bread, had even begun his 'second cup'.

Kirsty made a suggestion. "I've been thinking – it would be fine to take the bairns to the berry-hill. You could run some of us now, Arthur, and bring the rest when you come back to pick-up Davie. We'll just leave the dishes, Joey. Magnie can put the bread and butter and that under the dresser, so the cat doesn't get at it."

Arthur, pleased at some action at last, set off with his first load of passengers; Kirsty and Caro in the side-car, and Connie on the pillion. By the time he returned, Joey had prepared three empty jam-jars, a syrup-tin, and the small milk-pail, to hold any berries they might find, and Davie had just finished his tea. Joey, Marina and Jem, all squeezed into the side-car, Davie got on behind Arthur, and they started off with bone-shaking suddenness.

Where the north-bound road reached the top of the hill, the others were waiting for them, Kirsty sitting on a brae with her feet in the ditch, while the two girls hopped, impatiently, on and off the border-field.

Kirsty heaved herself to her feet as Joey and the children got out of the side-car. She shook her head as Arthur and Davie set off northwards and the clatter finally faded into the distance.

"I'd be stone-deaf in no time if I went far in that contraption," she remarked. "It's a wonder there isn't a law against it. There are laws that make less sense."

Joey silently agreed with her.

They left the road and began to walk over the springy heather. Overhead, the sky was an opalescent pearl and, away to the north-east, the sea lay still and almost colourless, broken here and there by tiny islets. Two red-throated divers flew high above, heading for the secluded western side of the island, and croaking plaintively.

Kirsty watched them for a moment. "'*When the raingoose flies to the hill, draw down your boats and go where you will*'," she quoted. "'*When the raingoose flies to the sea, draw up your boats and put them in lea*'. Well, it's fine enough at the moment."

The children had run on ahead, pausing every now and then to scramble about on bare knees, looking for the berry-heather, recognisable by its bright, yellowish-green colour.

Joey said, "I brought the milk-pail for us two to gather in."

Kirsty chuckled. "I doubt that if I get down on my hands and knees it'll take a block-and-tackle to get me up again. My, it's many a day since I was in the berry-hill last."

"It's beautiful here tonight," said Joey.

She looked round, at the pale sea with its tiny green-topped islands, and the voe, darkly-shadowed; the hills, dotted with slow-moving sheep and darting lambs; the straight white ribbons of smoke rising from the chimneys of the Wastervoe houses; the peace of a summer Sunday evening. It was beautiful, as she had remarked. But Joey was conscious of feeling strangely sad and alone; lonely, although Kirsty and the children were there with her. A forlorn feeling of not belonging there, or anywhere, of never belonging … She gave her head a little shake, imagining what Kirsty would say if she tried to put her foolish fancies into words.

She looked at Kirsty, who stood quite still, hands on hips, her features set in a rapt and tranquil immobility. Could it be that Kirsty, too, felt the strange, wild atmosphere of the hills? Joey was loathe to break the silence. For a moment, she and Kirsty seemed to be united in a mute understanding. Then Kirsty spoke.

"I'm sure that's Charlotte's old ewe over there, the one they called Yarma, for the tongue of her never lay. Bend down, Joey, until you can get her ears against the sky-line, and see if you can make out the mark. A piece out before and a rit behind, that's the Leabakka mark."

There was a smothered sound from Joey as she dropped down onto her knees. "Was that what you were looking at? The old ewe?"

"What other would I be looking at?" Kirsty replied, slightly puzzled, "and what are you laughing at, Joey?"

Joey, to Kirsty's satisfaction, confirmed that the ewe did indeed have the Leabakka mark on its ears, then she joined the children, leaving Kirsty sitting on the edge of an old peat-bank and scanning the hillside in an effort to pick out more sheep.

After a time, Caro turned a flushed and frowning face towards Joey, drawing the back of her hand across her forehead. "Oh, Joey, there's midges out!"

Connie, her face and bare arms speckled with pink spots, said, "I think we'll go home now."

"We're supposed to wait for Arthur, that was the arrangement," Joey told her.

"Oh no! That'll be hours yet," wailed Caro, pulling up a handful of heather and scrubbing it across her face in an effort to ease the discomfort.

"Oh, it isn't as bad as all that, Caro," Joey said, briskly, and untruthfully.

Marina and Jem appeared from behind a brae and began to add their lamentations to those of the two older girls. Kirsty was standing up now, fanning herself with a handkerchief.

"Let's see what your Mam says," suggested Joey. As she looked around, it seemed as if everything was faintly obscured by a thin, grey mist that quivered with the rapid movement of minute wings. Never could she remember seeing midges in such numbers.

"My, what a night of midges," said Kirsty. "Do you know, I'm sure I actually heard the hum of them! Likely nobody would believe me, but it's true enough."

"The bairns want to make for home." Joey glanced at Marina and Caro who were verging between tears and anger. Connie and Jem were taking it more calmly, but they looked both unhappy and uncomfortable.

"My dear, I think we'll have to go," said Kirsty. "The boys will surely understand that we've gone on."

They rejoined the road and began to walk homewards and still the midges were with them. On the hillside, the sheep were running in an effort to reduce their discomfort.

"Oh, for a breath of air," said Kirsty.

But all around there was stillness, the pale, cloudless sky, and the unmoving sea.

They reached home eventually. Joey had, at length, told the children to run on ahead, for neither Kirsty's age nor bulk were conducive to speed, and to the youngsters she seemed to be scarcely moving at all.

Even in the house, the midges made their presence felt, though to a lesser degree. Gaerd, who had bounded to meet them, gave a kind of smothered sneeze, rubbed clumsily at his nose with a paw, and then dived underneath the restin-shair. Magnie, who had been dozing in a chair by the fire, came to himself with a grunt, and hastily changed it into a cough as they entered.

"I ... I didn't hear the bike," he said.

"Oh, Magnie, we've nearly been eaten alive by the midges! I think I'll be the worse of this night," lamented Kirsty.

"You would seem to have brought them in with you," Magnie replied, reaching down his pipe from the mantelpiece.

"The very dab!" said Kirsty. "If the smoke from that doesn't put paid to them, nothing will."

Joey was examining the bitten faces of the girls. "Caro, don't scratch, you'll only make it worse. I wonder if some cold cream would help? It's all I can think of."

"Mercy bless you, let's try anything," said Kirsty.

The girls were so diverted by the spectacle of Kirsty standing in front of the mirror, carefully creaming her face for the first and last time, that they almost forgot their own discomfort.

It was past ten o'clock when Davie and Arthur returned. Arthur was very disgruntled. They had had a puncture on the road home, and petrol-trouble, besides which there hadn't been a sign of the Faroese yachtsman.

Joey, tidying up for the night, picked up the jars with the result of the berry-picking and tipped all the berries together into the pail. "I'll make some jam with them tomorrow. It will only be a spoonful for each of the bairns, but it will maybe please them."

Kirsty gingerly touched her face, where the pink midge-bites were still visible. "It was dear-bought jam," she said.

Chapter 14

JESSIE MARY PAYS A VISIT

B Y THE end of August, the peats were home and the hay was in, and then September was upon them and Magnie got the scythe out again and began to cut the corn. The weather was still and pleasant and the fields took on a mellow, golden hue, with the hills a warm, russet-brown.

But if Nature indulged in a mood of cheerful tranquillity, Kirsty did not, for the time of her cousin Jessie Mary's visit was drawing ever-nearer. The ben-end was ready and waiting, only needing the bed to be made. A fire was set on every afternoon and the flock mattress propped up on its side in front of it supported by chairs. A new pair of rose-coloured flannelette sheets had been ordered from Nina's club-book and lay in a brown-paper parcel on top of the wardrobe, together with the newly-starched valance and the pillowcases with the flower-embroidered ends.

The home-made, wooden wash-stand, which normally stood in the bedroom of Kirsty and Magnie, had been repainted and now stood in the window recess of the ben-end, holding the big porcelain basin with its design of pink roses.

As the time approached, Kirsty grew more and more agitated and unusually irritable. Joey knew, from past experience, that she would revert to normal once Jessie Mary actually arrived. It was the anticipation of the visit that seemed to upset her placidity and caused her to indulge in a frenzy of preparation. Jessie Mary was not one to hold her tongue if things were not as she thought they should be.

When the ben-end had been prepared to her satisfaction, Kirsty turned her attention to the living-room. "When is this ceiling going to be distempered?" she demanded, one evening, as they were having their tea.

Davie looked upward at the beams, his gaze coming to rest on the brownish discoloration directly above the Tilley lamp. "I'll need to find a moment, sometime," he answered, "when I've finished the new peat-bunker, in the porch …"

"Oh, you have enough on your hands," said Kirsty, summarily dismissing his tentative offer.

"Dad's been sawing wood for me, but I could manage without him for tonight …"

"Och, your father is an old man, he might fall and break his legs," replied Kirsty, ignoring Magnie's grunt of indignation. She fixed Arthur with a baleful eye. "There's nothing to stop you doing it, Arthur!"

Arthur looked gloomy, but resigned. He muttered something about "promising to play cards with the boys," the last, hopeless stand of one who is cornered.

Kirsty gave no sign of having heard the remark. After tea, she produced a large brush and a tin of white distemper. Arthur, with an expression of revulsion, put on the old boiler-suit belonging to his father, and which Kirsty had retrieved from some obviously musty source, and set to work. Joey began to spread newspapers over the furniture, a fortunate fore-sight, as the sound of paint splattering against them soon testified. Each time Arthur re-loaded his brush, and applied it to the rafters, there came a sound like a hail-storm.

Caro was sitting in the 'best' chair, with her legs dangling over one of the padded arms, trying to learn the poem she had been set for homework. "'*One I know, one I know, who has never seen the snow'*," she recited monotonously, then stopped to wipe a splodge of distemper from her cheek. "I can't get peace," she complained, and Arthur scowled at her.

"You've maybe never seen the snow, my bairn, but there's a good imitation of it in here tonight," said Kirsty, with heavy humour.

"I can't think why you had to ask the old faggot here," said Arthur, referring, presumably, to Jessie Mary.

"You'll be an old faggot yourself someday," answered Kirsty.

"There'll be no fun while she's here!" Arthur jabbed his brush viciously at an awkward corner between the beams.

Kirsty regarded the splattered newspapers, some of which had slipped to disclose white-spotted portions of furniture, penny-spots on the linoleum, even the wallpaper hadn't escaped unscathed.

"You've had enough fun tonight to last you for a while," she told him, grimly.

If Arthur wasn't looking forward to Jessie Mary's visit, neither was Joey, though for quite a different reason. She could imagine the sly prying, and the endless questions; Jessie Mary's curiosity was well-known. She recalled how, when a child, Jessie Mary would get her alone and then proceed to question her about household affairs under the pretence of having a friendly chat. How much had Magnie got for his calf at the roup? What had Kirsty paid for the new quilt on the ben bed? And, later on, was Davie courting again?

It had been bad enough when she had known nothing of these things, and cared less, but now there was her engagement, and wedding plans, for Jessie Mary to try to get her nose into. Could she hope to parry the questions, or give answers which wouldn't offend the old woman and bring repercussions on the whole family? Unlike Arthur, who had his job to go to during the day and who could spend the evenings on his own pursuits, she couldn't hope to keep out of Jessie Mary's way for much of the time.

If her original plans had materialised, she would have been married and in her own home by now. She caught herself up, stopping herself from thinking along those lines. Hugh's last letter had contained nothing to make her think that their marriage was any nearer. He hadn't even said when he expected to be home again. Sometimes, she wished Hugh would be a little more forthcoming for it made it difficult for her to answer even Kirsty's kindly enquiries. One of these days, she made up her mind suddenly, she would call on the Sutherlands, find out if they knew any more than she did.

But before she had the chance to do so, Jessie Mary had arrived, her tin box and fibre suitcase seeming to bear witness that her stay would be a prolonged one. Arthur happened to be at home when she came and, while Kirsty escorted her to the bedroom, he muttered to Joey and Magnie that they'd "be lucky to get rid of her by Christmas."

Jessie Mary was in her late sixties, a tall, spare woman with thin white hair scraped back from a bony face and screwed into a meagre bun. Her pale eyes were screened by hooded lids, giving her a slightly sinister appearance. The children would stand in awe of her for the first few days, fearing to find that pale, enigmatic eye regarding them, but then they would revert to normal and soon a state of hostility would result between the two factions, with the girls on one side, Jessie Mary on the other, and Kirsty and Joey the unfortunates in the middle.

One evening, when almost a week of Jessie Mary's visit had passed, Joey went over to Leabakka. She purposely chose an evening when she knew Jessie Mary had arranged a visit to Houll, otherwise she felt quite sure that Jessie Mary would have been ready to accompany her.

She reached the Leabakka gate when the light was softly diminishing into the blue-grey of twilight. The sunset had left little, triangular-shaped clouds of dull-gold and purple, all pointing north-west, like strange, motionless birds, and there was a crescent moon, high and pale, above the Wastervoe hills.

On the rigs below the house, the corn was being stooked, the two, dark figures of Johnny and his father visible only as moving shadows in the half-light. Soon they would have to stop working, for it would be too dark to see what they were doing.

The evening passed pleasantly. Joey felt relaxed and happy for the first time since Jessie Mary had descended on Grinda Garth. Johnny and Gibbie came in and had their eight o'clocks, then Johnny, now dressed in his second-best trousers and jacket, disappeared on some errand of his own.

Nina gave Joey a glance that was charged with meaning. "Off to the Burgoynes'!" she said, her voice low so that Charlotte, busily putting peats on the fire, wouldn't hear.

Charlotte straightened up, her face rosy from the heat of the fire. "Did Kirsty not think to come over with you?"

Joey shook her head. "I think she was glad to get the house to herself for an hour or two. Besides, if Jessie Mary was to come back from Houll and find that she wasn't in there might be ructions. Jessie Mary is always quick to take the huff."

"You don't need to tell me that!" Charlotte sat down and picked up her knitting. "No one would put up with that one unless her own."

Gibbie reached for a newspaper from the broad sill of the back window, and then sat down on a chair placed in front of the box-bed. He looked at Joey. "What's Magnie thinking about all this that's going on in the world? And this Hitler fellow?"

Joey, who hadn't troubled herself about it, couldn't remember if Magnie had expressed an opinion or not. It was all so far away, nothing that would affect any of them.

"I couldn't say," she answered, slowly, her mind on the pattern of the jumper she was knitting. Had she put daffodil where she ought to have put the lemon?

Gibbie opened the newspaper, and his blue eyes held a serious expression instead of their usual twinkle. "It's not good, not good," he said, sighing gustily, so that his white moustache quivered like a tuft of cotton-plant blown by the wind.

"Someone's coming in," said Nina, her keen ears detecting footsteps on the brigstanes outside the window.

It was Alexina Hoseason. She looked round the middle-door, timidly, and seemed a little taken aback to find Joey there, for her smile slowly diminished as she looked at her.

Charlotte, of course, was on her feet in a moment, bidding her to come in, and making a place for her on the end of the restin-shair nearest the fire.

"I've been posting letters, so I thought I'd drop along on my way home," said Alexina.

"Is Jessie Mary still beside you, at Houll, or has she made for Grinda Garth?" asked Joey.

Alexina's fingers plucked at the fringes of her scarf. "She was still there when I left."

Her uneasiness was so apparent that Joey wondered at it. She bent over her knitting to hide a smile. Probably Jessie Mary had been running-down everyone at Grinda Garth. That would be enough to upset the sensitive Alexina and make her feel uncomfortable and guilty.

When Alexina rose to go, Joey got up, too, for it was after ten o'clock. Nina went with them to the door.

"Have you got a torch, Joey? Seeing there's the two of you, I won't come over the grass with you. Mam and Dad have been out in the corn all day so I'm going to do the night-milking," Nina explained. "I'll probably have a run over to Grinda Garth tomorrow, Joey."

The two girls began to walk towards the road. "I hear that Janet and Sammy Irvine are getting married in December," remarked Joey, by way of conversation, for Alexina had fallen silent.

"Yes," Alexina replied, then added quickly, "Johnny wasn't in tonight. Over at the Burgoynes', I suppose. Is he going to make a match of it with Netta, do you think?"

It seemed to Joey that Alexina had deliberately changed the subject, steered it away from her sister's forthcoming wedding. She wondered why.

When Joey reached Grinda Garth she found that Jessie Mary had returned only minutes before. The cracked leatherette bag which contained her knitting was propped against the table-leg and she was divesting herself of her black coat and hat. She bore a strong resemblance to a skinny black crow. She was speaking to Kirsty, but paused as Joey came in, and her fingers became motionless on the top button of her coat. Her eyes, as she regarded Joey, had a strange glitter, and her thin lips were curved in a faint, malicious smile.

Joey knew that look, had seen it many times before when Jessie Mary had a particularly spiteful piece of gossip to impart. For an instant, it seemed as if her heart stopped beating, to start again with slow, painful thumps. Some sense told her that the old woman had some knowledge which directly affected her, and which would cause her distress.

But Jessie Mary was in no hurry to communicate whatever intelligence she possessed. All through supper, she gave vent to her usual tittle-tattle and ill-speaking, criticising the house-keeping methods at Houll; the fact that there had only been margarine on the table at tea-time; that the old man had placed his byre-boots beside her chair; and that Janet hadn't volunteered any information about her wedding-dress although she had "tried to draw her out." All the time, it seemed to Joey, that there was something more, something which pleased her, and which she was savouring as long as possible.

Joey began to clear away the supper things and then to wash the dishes. Magnie called Gaerd from under the restin-shair and went to shut him up in the barn for the night. Davie had retired to bed, for he had to be at work early in the morning. Arthur still hadn't come in. Kirsty began to lay down the embers on the hearthstone, preparatory to 'resting' the fire.

"You'd better get away to your bed, Jessie," Kirsty suggested. "You'll be tired after your outing."

"Oh, I'll just sit here for a moment and warm my feet," Jessie Mary answered. She gave Joey a sly, side-long glance. "You never told me that you'd given up the house of Hivdalea, Joey," she said.

"What?" Prepared as she was for something of the kind, the shock of the actual words seemed to stun Joey.

Kirsty put down the tongs with a clatter. "Who told you that?" she demanded of Jessie Mary.

"Oh, Sammy Irvine came up to Houll tonight. He came to tell Janet that he'd got word that he could get Hivdalea, seeing Hugh Sutherland had given it up. Did you know, Joey?"

"My mercy, of course she knew," Kirsty said, briskly, picking up the peat-basket. "Och – it needs such a lot done to it. The cost would be more than the honour."

"Sammy and Janet seem well-pleased to get it," sniffed Jessie Mary.

"I hope it keeps fine for them!" replied Kirsty, with unwonted sarcasm. "Here, Joey, you get the resting-peats, you're abler than I am."

Joey took the basket, knowing quite well that Kirsty's tart words had been an excuse to get her away from Jessie Mary's sharp eyes and malicious tongue. She took as long as possible to find suitable peats, and when she returned to the living-room Jessie Mary had disappeared, no doubt hustled off by Kirsty.

She put down the basket and went back to wiping the table. No words were spoken but the atmosphere was electric. Then Kirsty said agitatedly, "Did you know, Joey?"

Joey shook her head.

"Then I told Jessie Mary a lie, and the Good Man forgive me, but I wasn't going to have her tormenting you," said Kirsty, firmly, and with no sign of remorse. She added, "Did Hugh not mention it in his last letter?"

"No. But Hugh doesn't tell me much about anything," said Joey, a tinge of bitterness in her tone.

"Oh well, I daresay he'll have a good explanation for it," said Kirsty.

Joey knew that the words were simply to make her feel better, that Kirsty didn't really believe in Hugh's sincerity. Neither did she, any more.

Chapter 15

MAGNIE'S PURCHASE

THE sale of old Leebie Manson's belongings took place shortly afterwards. Magnie, who rarely went anywhere had, for some unknown reason, set his mind on attending the sale. Kirsty was torn between amusement and concern.

"Don't you go spending your money on trash now," she admonished him. "We're not needing any pictures of the Gospel ship or Bonnie Prince Charlie, mind."

On the morning of the sale, she asked Joey if she was going with Magnie, "for the sake of somebody to keep an eye on him."

Joey thought about old Leebie's pathetic bits-and-pieces and shook her head. "There's no need to worry, Auntie Kirsty, there won't be anything there that will fetch more than a few shillings."

Davie, coming in at that moment, overheard. "They say there's to be some stuff sold belonging to the Wesleyan minister who's leaving Sandayre," he told them.

"What did I tell you? Magnie is sure to come home with a bunch of framed tracts!" Kirsty threw up her hands in despair.

Davie laughed. "I'm thinking to go down to the sale myself."

Kirsty's expression relaxed a little. "Then don't you let him bid on useless rubbish."

"I don't think there's any fear of that, Mam."

Joey and Kirsty had the house to themselves for the girls had set off with their father and grandfather and Jessie Mary was spending the day at Leabakka. Charlotte had felt duty-bound to invite her for the whole day, at least once, and Jessie Mary had chosen that particular Saturday and had left immediately after breakfast.

It was late afternoon when Magnie, Davie and the children returned. Kirsty sighted them as they appeared at the top of the road and she pressed her face close to the window and peered out intently.

"They don't appear to be carrying much, mercy be praised," she said, her voice echoing back hollowly from the pane.

Joey put down her knitting and began to wind up the balls of coloured wool lying at her feet. "They'll be famished. I'll see about the tea, although it's early."

The children came bursting in through the doorway, bringing the bracing tang of fresh air with them.

"I'm hungry," announced Connie.

"Is the tea not ready yet?" asked Caro, pulling off her melton-cloth coat and throwing it over the restin-shair.

Magnie and Davie arrived in a more leisurely manner, Davie echoing his daughter's words, "Is the tea not ready yet?"

Kirsty was bending down to pull open the dresser-door. "Boy, you can surely wait ten minutes! It's not five o'clock yet."

"Well, it's just that we have to go back and we don't want it to be too dark before we get there."

"Go back? What are you going back for?" demanded Kirsty, straightening up with the basin of bannocks in her hand.

"To fetch the stuff we bought. It's standing outside, and it looks to me as if it might come a shower or two."

Kirsty began to pile bannocks onto the pink plate with the trellis-work round the edges. "Could you not just have brought it back with you, instead of making another trip over it?"

"We came to get the mare and cart," said Magnie.

Kirsty's lips moved but it was some time before she found the power of speech. "The mare and cart? Magnie Mouat! Just what have you gotten up to the day?"

"Oh, Mam, it's all right, it's only …" began Davie.

Kirsty turned on him. "After all I said, Davie! Could you not have looked better after your father?"

Magnie, unexpectedly roused and hardly able to get a word in, circumscribed circles in the air with his pipe, and stuttered, "It's … it's … some of it belongs to Davie …"

"Is that so? Like father, like son, a true-said word! A poor thing if my eye has to be on you all the time."

"Oh … I … I'll go and yoke up the mare till this tea is ready." Magnie moved with unusual speed towards the door, making a strategical withdrawal, and Davie followed.

Kirsty kept up her scolding all through tea and even after the men had departed. Arthur arrived, and the tale of woe had to be repeated. Arthur listened with no great show of interest until, at the end, he said, "I wonder what they've bought?"

"Likely some old, worm-eaten table! Or maybe the parrot's cage!" Kirsty predicted, for Leebie had had a parrot which had died the previous year. Joey recalled to herself how upset the old woman had been at the time, but Joey felt glad now that the bird had died, for who would have given it a home?

The Tilley was lit, and the curtains drawn, but the girls kept parting them to peer out into the gathering darkness. Kirsty had questioned them as to what their father and grandfather had bought but, it seemed, they had spent much of the time playing on the beach. They were as much in the dark as anyone else.

Gradually, Kirsty's ire was replaced by a mild curiosity. "Any sign of the wanderers returning?" she would ask from time to time.

Marina was watching from the window when they at last came in sight, dark silhouettes against the still-light sky. She dropped the curtain and sped for the porch.

"Don't you run out, now, in your slippers," commanded Kirsty.

"I'm only going to stand in the door, Mam."

Caro and Connie were close behind her. Joey and Kirsty exchanged glances, and waited.

Davie came in carrying an oblong, wooden box which he placed on the table, then turned it round, so that they could see the fabric-covered speaker at the top, the dial below, and the three large, black knobs below that.

"It's a wireless!" Caro clasped her hands in ecstasy.

"My, Davie!" breathed Kirsty, almost as rapt as the child.

"There's two accumulators with it, and a grid bias battery, but we'll have to get a high-tension battery from the shop on Monday, then we'll be all set," Davie said, proudly. "Look, this is the on-off switch, and this one is the reaction – oh, and we'll need to get an aerial put up, outside …"

"I'll give you a hand with that," Arthur said, promptly. "We can put the pole at the bottom of the kale-yard."

Davie was making for the door again. "I'll have to give Dad a hand with the rest of the stuff."

Kirsty was busy examining the wireless from every angle. Arthur had removed the back, and now she stared in at the array of wires, valves, and various bits-and-pieces.

"My. Why they call it a wireless I'll never know, for it seems to be nothing but wires! Should there not be more to it, Arthur? Maybe half of it's never here, for Davie would know no better. I doubt it'll need something more to make it work."

"Oh, Mam! It only needs to be connected up."

"Mm, we'll see," Kirsty still sounded doubtful.

She turned round as there came a scuffling of feet in the porch, and Davie appeared, backwards, through the doorway. He was carrying one end of something that was large and heavy and he was delivering instructions to Magnie who was, presumably, at the other end.

"Take your end a bit more to the right – that's fine, steady as she goes – now lift up – watch the door-jamb! Yes, we'll do it, I think …"

"My mercy, what's this now?" Kirsty exclaimed.

The structure was finally manoeuvred through the door and seen to be of dark, polished wood, with a good deal of ornamentation, and two pedals covered in fawn jaspe linoleum. Magnie lowered the end to the floor and mopped his face with a large red handkerchief.

Kirsty breathed heavily. "Magnie Mouat, have you taken leave of your senses? That's an organ!"

"I know that!" replied Magnie, a little testily.

"There's a piece to go on the top," said Davie. "It's all fancy, with fretwork, and a sort of case in the middle to hold the music books. It's still out in the cart. Come and give me a lift in with it, Arthur."

"Can you tell me what use we have for an organ in this house?" Kirsty was demanding, grimly.

"Well, the bairns might learn to play," Magnie said, slowly. Then he suddenly squared his shoulders, looked her straight in the eye, and said, "It's not for you, Kirsty! It's for Joey, there."

Joey had been gazing at the organ, not saying a word. Now, she looked at Magnie in some astonishment. "You remembered, Uncle Magnie!"

Magnie cleared his throat and looked uncomfortable. "I minded you used to play when you were a bairn, before you came to us. I thought maybe you'd like to take it up again – so I thought I'd have a bid on the organ!"

"That's true, Joey, you could play," Kirsty began, then stopped. The thoughtful expression on her face denoted that something was crossing her mind. Then she continued, briskly, "Well, well. The place for it is ben, but it can't go there while Jessie Mary is beside us, so we'll need to find somewhere else, for the moment."

For Kirsty had suddenly realised that Magnie must have read the sale list, had seen the organ mentioned, and determined to buy it for Joey. It was his way of trying to make up for the non-fulfilment of her plans for Hivdalea, and for the disillusionment she must have suffered over Hugh. But he would be mortified if he thought that anyone had guessed.

Kirsty's eyes suddenly misted over and she turned away quickly so that no one would notice. Magnie was a good man. Not that she had ever doubted it, but sometimes it was brought home to her so forcibly that she was filled with remorse at her own sharp tongue. Though, she felt certain, Magnie never noticed her tartness. He was too guileless, too – too good! Yes, too good for me, too good for any of us, she thought with sudden humility.

She sniffed, loudly, and Joey said, with some concern, "Are you starting with a cold, Auntie Kirsty?"

"Och, it's just dust out of the wireless," Kirsty replied, quickly. "Now, if we push the table nearer to the restin-shair there might be room for the organ, longways, in the corner there."

Davie and Arthur came back, carrying the ornamental top, and Davie pointed out the music-compartment. It contained two fat books – *Redemption Songs* and *Sankey's 1,300 Pieces*. Joey flicked them over, saw that they were set in sol-fa, and remembered, with startling clarity, her mother sitting by her side in her grandparents' house at Snarrafirth, showing her the scales, helping her pick out simple hymns on the old organ with the sticky keys and leaky bellows. They had had no organ of their own or she would have brought it with her to Grinda Garth. It gave her a warm feeling to think that Uncle Magnie had remembered.

She rolled back the lid and looked at the keys, mellowed to a deep ivory with the years, and felt the urge to play again, to hear the sonorous notes of the bass blend with the high treble.

The children were hovering at her elbow. "Play, Joey," Caro was insisting. "Go on, play!"

Suddenly, Joey no longer wanted to play. It had been so long. Probably she had forgotten all she had ever learned and there would be a pitiful crash of inharmonious sound when she touched the keys. But she could learn all over again, that she promised herself.

"Play that song we're learning at school," said Marina. "*Here we go gathering nuts in May*. Do you know it, Joey?"

"No, give me a hymn-book, I'll find a good one," Connie put in.

They heard the thud as the porch-door closed. Kirsty shut her eyes. "Jessie Mary!"

"Then that settles it," Joey pulled down the lid, reflecting that it was the only time she had been glad to hear the return of Jessie Mary.

Magnie grabbed his cap from the arm of the chair, muttering something about "seeing to the mare." Davie cast a trapped look round the room, but could find no excuse for leaving it. Arthur remained unmoved. He went back to the table, replaced the back on the wireless, and said, "We'll need to put up a shelf, Davie. One that can hold the accumulator at the side."

Jessie Mary came in, her mouth set in mulish lines, and Kirsty immediately surmised that Charlotte had not held her tongue over something or other and had brought a hornet's nest about her ears.

"You've come, Jessie," Kirsty addressed her. "I'll put on the kettle. I wasn't expecting you for an hour's time yet."

"I thought I'd been long enough," Jessie Mary said, stiffly.

"Did you come on your own? Joey could have met you …"

"Nina came as far as the gate with me. I told her she needn't bother to come in."

Kirsty looked at her, speculatively. "That's a pity. We'd have been glad to see her."

Jessie Mary's glance fell on the organ and her mouth dropped open. "What's this? A new bit of furniture you've been getting, Kirsty?"

"Oh, it's an organ Magnie has bought at the sale," Kirsty began to measure tea into the pot from the red and black canister.

"You never told me he was going to buy it!" Jessie Mary's tone was accusing.

Kirsty took the knitted pot-holder from the hook at the side of the mantelpiece and lifted the kettle from above the flames before she answered. "Did I not? We're hoping some of the bairns will take an interest in it and, of course, Joey can play," she said, unblushingly.

It wasn't lies, she told herself, though she knew she was deliberately misleading Jessie Mary, allowing her to think that she had known, and approved, of Magnie's decision to buy the organ.

She sighed as she poured the water into the pot. It would be as well when Jessie Mary went. Jessie Mary was having a bad influence on her.

Chapter 16

AN OUT-STAYED WELCOME

THE days dragged on into October and still Jessie Mary remained at Grinda Garth. She went out visiting less now for the majority of the Aestervoe families had done or said something which had given her cause for offence. Few had been able to take her malicious gossip and spiteful tongue and remain silent.

The atmosphere at Grinda Garth was strained, to say the least. Joey wondered how they had avoided the pitfalls and hadn't succeeded in slighting Jessie Mary, unintentionally.

Kirsty had no doubts – Jessie Mary knew when she was well off!

A letter had come from Hugh explaining why he had given up the lease of Hivdalea. It would be an expensive business to put it in a proper state of repair now he understood that he wouldn't be eligible for a Board grant; besides, one day the house on Gardie Hill would be his, and it seemed extravagant to waste money on a house they would probably only occupy for a few years. He added that he was sorry he hadn't consulted her first, it had slipped his memory, but he was sure she would understand and agree that it was the best to do.

Joey had re-folded the letter and replaced it in the envelope. She hadn't tried to analyse her feelings; she could not have said whether she understood, or agreed. One thing she did know, she would never share a house with May and Belle Sutherland.

As the weather became colder and the nights began to draw in, the children were able to play outside less and less. By the time they got home from school it was lamp-lighting time and after tea it was quite dark. Often, Jem came up to 'play', for Willa had little desire for the child's company, and Jem, though of a quiet nature, couldn't be expected to conform to Willa's stringent regulations. Once Sydney was asleep, she mustn't pull a chair across the floor, rattle her cup against the saucer, cough, drop a pencil.

There were no such rules at Grinda Garth, but none of the children were given to being rowdy and things had always gone smoothly. But not any longer. Jessie Mary couldn't abide an occasional shriek of childish laughter, and when, after being rebuked, the laughter subsided into giggles, Jessie Mary declared that they were "making a fool of her."

"It seems to me," said Caro who, of the four, felt the most constrained, "that we aren't even supposed to breathe!"

"Old people are like that," Joey picked her words carefully. "We have to make allowances."

"Mam isn't!" Caro pointed out. "Least she wasn't, until old Jessie Mary came."

"Well, we'll just have to put up with it until she goes," Joey sighed.

It was a dull time of year for the children, at best, for summer holidays were already a memory and Christmas seemed an equally long time ahead. Even the anticipation of the Hallowe'en party didn't cheer them, this year. No one could see any future other than an endless winter with Jessie Mary always there.

On a never-to-be-forgotten afternoon, Joey found herself alone with Jessie Mary. Kirsty, who had been suffering from neuralgia, had taken aspirin and had gone to lie down for a couple of hours. Jessie Mary, perched comfortably in the 'best' chair, began to talk. Joey, who knew she would need all her time if she was to get her knitting completed and ready to be sold at the weekend, had seated herself in the restin-shair, as far away from Jessie Mary as possible, hoping to discourage conversation.

"My, it's peaceful with just you and me, Joey," Jessie Mary began, ingratiatingly,

"We'd get on fine, just the two of us. When you get married, and have your own home, maybe I'll come and visit you once in a while."

Joey bent her head, matching the colours in the Fair Isle pattern, and muttered something indistinguishable.

"It'll not be long now, will it? Christmas, maybe?"

"Oh well, nothing's settled ..."

"Hugh is coming home then, isn't he?"

"I couldn't say ..."

"Oh! Did you not know? I happened to speak with his mother at the kirk on Sunday, and she told me, so it's true enough."

Joey saw the side-long, calculating glance of Jessie Mary's pale eyes, and drew in her breath sharply. "I don't think Hugh's plans are all that cut-and-dried," she said, firmly. "It all depends on how long this trip takes."

"Is that so? Well, that's what his mother told me." But Jessie Mary didn't sound quite so sure of herself now.

For a moment or two there was only the sound of the American clock on the mantelpiece. Then Jessie Mary returned to the subject with vigour.

"Now I come to think of it, your cousin Johnny said the same thing the last day I was over there. He said that Netta Burgoyne's brother was coming home just before Christmas, and that he was on the same ship as Hugh Sutherland, the *Ben Nevis*, is that not right, Joey ?"

"Hugh is on the *Ben Nevis*, yes."

"That's what Johnny said. You ask Nina!" Jessie Mary was triumphant.

Joey laid aside her knitting. "It's time I was going with the hens' corn, and shutting them in."

"They've just well had their dinner," Jessie Mary said, sourly.

Joey let herself out into the cold, windy October day.

She didn't spare a glance for the late flowers which made the garden bright as flame; the lemon and bronze dahlias, the marigolds, the orange and scarlet nasturtiums, and the brilliant spikes of montbretia with its bronze-green leaves.

She fed the hens who had come running at the sight of her, throwing down handfuls of grain onto the hen-house floor. She knew Jessie Mary was capable of half-truths, just to draw her out, but she had said "ask Nina," therefore … But Joey knew that she would not be asking Nina. It would be embarrassing for both of them.

She counted the hens twice, got the right number, and closed the door, putting the wooden bar in position and sliding the cover over the opening at the bottom of the door where the hens went out and in. She remembered that she hadn't checked to see if there were any late eggs, but she didn't go back. There probably wouldn't be, anyway, for the old hens were losing their feathers and the chickens wouldn't start to lay before January.

Joey leaned for a moment against the dry-stone wall of the hen-house, unwilling to go back to the house, and Jessie Mary. A freshening wind ruffled the firth, putting little dabs of white on the grey. The sky had clouded over, so that the line where sky and sea met was barely discernible. She reflected on past autumn evenings when the anticipation of getting indoors on such a night had been more desirable; the firelight flickering rosily on the whitened chimney-sides, Kirsty setting out the tea things while keeping an eye on the Tilley which was in the process of being lit, the torch clasped round the vapouriser and sending up a bluish flame as the methylated spirit burned.

None of that was important now beside the figure of Jessie Mary crouched in her chair like an old witch. As Joey reached the porch door, the first raindrops struck hard against her cheek

The girls had returned from school, and Kirsty was up and looking more like her normal self now the aspirin had taken effect. Jessie Mary, looking grim, was disentangling her wool from round Marina's Wellingtons, for Marina never looked where she was going and had made a rush across the floor taking, as Kirsty put it, "all before her." It was not a cheerful scene, and later, when everyone was in and settled for the evening, there was none of the old contentment which had prevailed in Grinda Garth on wild, wet evenings.

The children settled down at the table with a game of tiddly-winks and it wasn't long before a stray counter rattled against Jessie Mary's knitting-needles.

"Tch, tch!" Jessie Mary shook her skirt and the counter fell on to the rag rug to be retrieved by Marina. "Can't you bairns keep your trash in one place? When I was your age I was having to spin and card and help my mother. I didn't have time to waste like the bairns nowadays."

"We were all the same, as far as that goes," Kirsty said, dryly, "but we always found a moment for our bits of toys, such as they were."

Jessie Mary sniffed. "You can count yourself well off, then. My conscience would never allow me to spend time capering like a merry-andrew."

Kirsty gave a tug at her wool which sent the ball half-way across the floor. "It's a poor heart that never rejoices."

The girls were whispering, their heads close together, Caro's and Marina's dark locks on either side of Connie's light-brown head. New rules for tiddly-winks were being discussed.

"If we hit Jessie Mary then that means an extra shot …"

"And if someone hits her twice running then they've won!"

Connie giggled, her only contribution, as she didn't possess the imagination of her younger sisters.

Soon coloured counters were flying across the room, fortunately (though not from the girls' point of view) none of them coming in contact with Jessie Mary's person. Kirsty and Joey were both well aware of what the girls were up to. They tried, discreetly, to give them discouraging glances, but the children were far too excited to be stopped by anything other than tougher measures.

Then Marina scored an unexpected hit on Jessie Mary's ear, and a second or two later the light in the room suddenly dimmed as Caro sent a counter through the Tilley mantle. Davie put down his newspaper and got up, slowly. The girls quickly got into more sedate positions on their chairs and eyed him, silently and apprehensively.

"We've had enough of this," he said. "Off upstairs to your beds."

"But, Dad, it's Friday night!" There were three cries of protest, for on Fridays they were allowed to stay up later than usual as there was no school the following day.

"You should have thought of that before," Davie pointed to the door. "Don't make me have to tell you again."

It wasn't often that Davie exerted his parental authority but, when he did, the girls knew that there was really no point in arguing. They would never get him to back down. And so they went, a forlorn trio, all their boisterous fun wiped away in a second. Davie sat down and picked up his paper again.

"I'll bring up some milk and biscuits in five minutes," Joey called after them.

The episode gave Jessie Mary a not-to-be-missed opportunity for airing her opinions on the upbringing of children. She complained with satisfaction until half-past ten, when she went to bed, saying that her head "was reeling."

"And no wonder," Kirsty said, grimly, as she heard the ben door click shut. "My own head isn't far off it, either, listening to her plootering on all night." She leaned forward and looked at Joey, "I very nearly told her that if the bairns annoyed her so much she'd be better off in her own home."

"It's a pity you didn't," answered Joey, feeling that she had had as much as she could stand of Jessie Mary, that day.

Kirsty shook her head. "It's a mercy I held my tongue. She's an awkward body to put up with, but she has nobody of her own, and that's a poor state to be in. If she was dead and gone tomorrow, I doubt if there's anybody who would care." Kirsty sighed, and lay back against the cushion of her chair. "Likely she'll set off one of these days and it'll be a Lord's mercy."

"There's not much signs of it," said Joey. "She runs all of us, you know. We can't do this or that, for sake of Jessie Mary."

Joey's voice was unexpectedly bitter and Kirsty eyed her keenly. "That's maybe true. Likely we shouldn't give in to her so much but, oh Joey, I feel I'm not able for her tantrums and it's anything for peace."

"It's her spiteful tongue I can't stand. I sometimes wonder how much longer it'll be before I break out and say something nasty to her."

Kirsty gave a half-laugh. "Oh, my bairn, we all feel the same! But I doubt if it would make any difference, she's thick-skinned when she wants to be. Both Caro and Arthur have been pretty straight with some of their remarks!"

"Is there no way … no one else she could go to?"

"Plenty she could go to, none who would want her," Kirsty said, bluntly. "I think we'll just have to struggle on, my Joey, and hope for the best."

Joey wasn't cheered any by this philosophy. It seemed a vain hope. There seemed to be no way in which they could rid themselves of the guest who had out-stayed her welcome.

Chapter 17

MAGNIE SPLASHES OUT

SOMETIME, during each autumn, a regatta for model yachts was held at the loch of Siglur which lay just over the crest of the hill above Aestervoe. Davie and Arthur were keen enthusiasts, out-fitting their yacht *Fram* with meticulous care, and pressing Joey into service to sew suits of sails.

The day before the regatta was to be held, Arthur was told that he would be needed to be one of the crew of the sixern which ferried goods from the inter-island steamer. It appeared that one of the regular crew had broken an arm so Arthur was required to substitute. Davie and Arthur discussed this hitch in their plans anxiously. It needed two to sail the yacht, one stationed at each end of the loch.

"It's a pity not to sail her. After all, we hold one of the cups," Davie said. "I'd have liked to have had a try at winning it outright."

"If the steamer comes early, I might get away in time," Arthur said, doubtfully.

"But there are lambs being shipped just now and I expect she'll be late."

Magnie removed his pipe from his mouth. "Maybe I could manage?" he suggested. "I was going up to watch anyway."

"Oh, that'll be fine then," Davie looked relieved. "It's just to turn the boat and set it on course …"

"Oh, I've done it before, in my younger days," Magnie reminded him.

The Saturday of the model yacht regatta turned out fine, but dull, with a strong south-west breeze. Davie and Magnie set out after breakfast, taking with them a bag of bannocks and a thermos of tea.

"Hmph! That's the last we'll see of them till dark nights," remarked Kirsty.

"They could have been better employed," Jessie Mary said, with a sniff.

No one answered her. Kirsty went into the porch to strain the milk, while Joey set about making the hens' feed.

Jessie Mary sniffed again and took up her knitting, ignoring the unwashed dishes stacked on the table and the fact that her own bed was unmade.

In the afternoon, the children were allowed to go to the loch to watch, Kirsty's warnings ringing in their ears.

"Don't go near the water, now! Mind and keep your mittens on. And keep away from the mires! They're deep enough in places to swallow up a horse and cart and never leave a trace!"

"Oh, alright, Mam," Caro muttered in exasperation. "We know!"

"Well, mind you don't forget, then." She watched as they set off across the field towards the hill fence. "I hope they'll be alright," she said, turning to Joey. "Their father is there, but I doubt if he'll be aware of anything other than that boat of his. Still, Magnie will keep an eye on them, I expect. He won't get as carried away as Davie."

When the house had been tidied, Joey began to iron her frock for the dance at night. It was the beige dress she had meant for her trousseau but, somehow, it had become her 'best' dress during the summer.

Arthur came home about three, threw his oilskins in the door, and immediately set out for the loch. The day was less pleasant now. The wind was rising and, in the garden, the withered flowers and grass rustled wildly. The sky was heavy, the firth a blue-grey smoke, and the outer isles were continually being obscured by sleety showers passing across them.

Kirsty came in from 'putting by' the cows. "No signs of our ones yet and I think the rain is not far off." She began to untie her shawl with fingers that were cold and red. "I'll be glad to sit down at the fire tonight."

"I could have seen to the animals," said Joey.

"Yes, and got yourself half frozen and you going to the dance," Kirsty replied, briskly.

Jessie Mary looked up with an acid smile. "I don't doubt she'll catch her death anyway if she goes out in that frock to a draughty hall. Have you got a pair of warm combinations to wear under it, Joey?"

Joey bent her head to hide a smile. "Well, no …"

"Och, lasses don't wear combinations nowadays," said Kirsty.

Jessie Mary sniffed as usual. "Combinations and open-drawers and two or three petticoats, one cotton, one flannel, and one knitted – that's what was worn in my day. But young folk are far too vain for that, though what's so clever about going round half-naked, I never can see. It'll lead to something, all this lack of modesty."

"No doubt," Kirsty said, sardonically. "Just as it did in our day!"

Jessie Mary sniffed again, "'*Vanity, vanity, all is vanity*' as the psalmist said."

Kirsty doubted if the psalmist had said anything of the kind, but not being certain of her ground, she elected to remain silent. Instead, she went out into the porch and opened the door, staring towards the dark hill, hoping to see that the regatta was over and that people were making for their homes. There were a few figures wending their way down the hill. Their progress was erratic, as they avoided the peat-banks and the many small fissures with which the hill was scarred. It was too dark, now, to be able to tell with any certainty who they were but at least it looked as if both yachtsmen and spectators were on the move.

Kirsty closed the door, well pleased, and went back into the living-room and began to build up the fire.

A little later they heard running feet on the brigstanes and the girls burst into the room, rosy-faced and gasping.

"Ooh, it's cold! My feet are frozen!"

"The cold's gone under my nails, Mam!"

"My rubber boots are leaking!"

"Daddy won two cups! And a third prize!"

"Well, well," Kirsty was unmoved. "You'd best get to the fire and get warmed. Connie, if your boots are leaking take your socks off as well. Joey'll find you a dry pair."

"There were ever so many boats on the loch."

"Uncle Gibbie used his staff to hook his boat ashore."

"Arthur's cap blew off and struck a boat's mast."

"And Daa – Daa went to jump across the narrow end of the loch – and he fell in!" Caro almost choked with mirth as she gave this information.

"He made a huge splash, and Sammy Irvine said the waves he made swamped his boat ..." Marina joined in.

Kirsty gave them her full attention. "What's all this you're saying? Daa fell in?"

Connie answered, for Caro and Marina were doubled up in paroxysms of laughter. "He got soaked."

"And where is he now? Did he not think fit to come and get his wet clothes off?"

Kirsty was worried now.

"Yes, Dad said we were to run home. The races were over, anyway. They're coming on behind."

Kirsty made for the stairs. "I'll need to get dry clothes to the fire, to air."

The garments were all arrayed above and around the hearth by the time the men arrived. The interlock underwear – the long drawers and the half-sleeved vest – hanging over the brass rod below the mantelpiece; the grey flannel shirt and second-best trousers spread over the backs of chairs turned towards the blazing fire.

Arthur and Davie had gone to the barn with the yacht, while Magnie came on to the house by himself. He presented a strange appearance. His dungaree trousers and jacket clung to him, with here and there a trace of some green and slimy weed. He was bare-headed, the bushy white hair for once lying sleekly against his head, and at each step his boots squeaked horribly.

Kirsty rounded on him. "I'll tell you this, Magnie Mouat, you're worse than a bairn!"

"Och, Kirsty …"

"Upstairs this minute and get changed! And why do you have your cap in your hand? Could it not be on your head where it belongs?"

Magnie held out his rolled-up cap and watched as a drop fell from it onto the floor, "Well, it was wet …"

"Hmph! So I see. There's surely not a dry rag on you. You've made a fine spectacle of yourself today." Kirsty began to gather up the dry clothes, tossing them one by one over her arm.

Magnie sat down on the chair nearest the door and began to haul off his boots. He looked glum.

Kirsty watched him, and suddenly her lips began to twitch. Then she began to laugh, rocking backwards and forwards.

Magnie scowled. "What are you laughing at, woman? I've maybe caught my death of cold."

Kirsty went on laughing. "Dear a dear! For a grown man to – I wish I'd seen it."

"You'll all be laughing on the other sides of your faces when I'm down with double pneumonia." For one of the few times in his life, Magnie was in a captious mood, feeling himself ill-done-by and vastly uncomfortable, physically. That Kirsty should laugh at him – Kirsty, of all people – was the last straw!

"I'm sure I'm not laughing," put in Jessie Mary. "If I was Kirsty, I'd give you something to think about. Coming home in that state!"

"What do you mean? What state? I'm only wet, what's wrong with that?" Magnie demanded, now completely roused.

"Look at the condition of the floor, for one thing. There's a pool of water running under the table, and all those muddy footprints … !" She gave a smirk, "Who's going to clean that up, do you think? It won't be you!"

Magnie gave an ironic laugh. "And it won't be you, that's sure. You've done precious little in the way of work in this house!"

"Magnie! Magnie!" reproved Kirsty, still struggling to control her amusement.

"Old besom! Coming in here with her gossip and ill-speaking, dressing down a man in his own house. Well, I've had enough of it!" Magnie thumped the table with his fist, rattling the tea cups which Joey had just set out, and causing one to roll onto the floor where it smashed into pieces.

Magnie snatched the clothes which Kirsty was still holding and stumped off towards the stairs in his sock feet.

Joey picked up the broken cup and threw the pieces into the ash-hole in the hearth.

"I'll need to get another cup out," she murmured to herself. Magnie's outburst had had a stunning effect on her, so that her movements and thoughts seemed to be automatic.

"You never need!" Jessie Mary was rolling up her knitting, her brows drawn down, her thin lips twisted angrily. "I'll not be staying, seeing I'm so little thought of."

Kirsty wiped her eyes with the corner of her apron and tried to make her expression more serious. "What are you saying, Jessie?"

"Magnie has made it very plain that I'm not wanted here, so I won't bother you any longer. I'll just make tracks for my own home. My, it's hard to be a lonely old body. I'm sure I've always tried to do my best, and tried to please everybody, though that's a hard task with some …" Jessie Mary tried to squeeze a few tears from her cold eyes, found it was impossible, and gave a gusty sigh instead.

"I'll speak to Magnie," said Kirsty.

"You never need! Joey, you'll maybe help me to pack my bits and pieces."

"Of course I will, but … but do you have to go?" Joey, having longed for Jessie Mary's departure, now felt some remorse, although she knew it to be unjustified. She also felt the need to renew Jessie Mary's invitation, even though the words almost stuck in her throat. Hospitality demanded it.

But it was with relief that she heard Jessie Mary say, "I'll go to my cousin Harriet at Selliwick. She'll be glad of my company. Like myself, she's alone in the world, poor soul."

Joey felt that her duty was done, she need try no more persuasions. If only nothing happened to make Jessie Mary change her mind again!

Upstairs, Kirsty was facing a still indignant Magnie. "You shouldn't have spoken like that, Magnie. Now she's in the huff."

"She can please herself!" Magnie buttoned up the grey flannel shirt and glowered, unrepentant.

"She says she's going."

"Good riddance."

"Would you not say you didn't mean it, ask her to stay a while longer?"

"No, I would not! It's not often I put my foot down Kirsty, but I'm doing it this time. There's been no peace in this house since that woman came. She complains about the bairns and since we got the wireless fixed up she's complained about that, and as for the organ I bought for Joey – she's never had a chance to lay a finger on it! So I hope the old besom takes the hint and goes." It was an unusually long speech for Magnie.

"It's not a lie you're saying," Kirsty agreed. "Well, I'll go back down and see what lay she's on now."

Jessie Mary made her departure the following morning. She was stiffly polite to Magnie, who made no attempt to get back into her good books, and she took a warm farewell of Kirsty, hinting that she knew she didn't have her sorrows to seek with the husband she'd got.

"Well, well," said Kirsty, non-committally, "drop us a line when you get settled in, Jessie. So, ta-ta, lass."

Jessie Mary climbed aboard the mail-car, while Joey handed her case to the driver. They watched the mail-car rattle up the main road, then started for home.

"*When – we all get married – we'll have saus – ages – for tea*," sang Kirsty, tunelessly, as she and Joey climbed the rough road to Grinda Garth.

Chapter 18

CRISIS FOR JEM

"ANOTHER one! Another one!" shrieked Caro, lying on her knees in the restin-shair and looking out of the window.

"How many is that, Caro? How many, now?" Marina rose to her feet in her excitement.

"Forty-two! Forty-two trawlers and four drifters."

"Marina Mouat! Is that you standing to your feet on the cushions with your slippers on?" Kirsty's voice came indignantly from the table where she was baking.

Without looking at her grandmother, or answering, Marina slid down again to her knees. Kirsty went on rolling out the dough for the bannocks, using the bottle she kept for the purpose.

Outside, a southerly gale gusted round the house and the voe was a tumbling mass of grey, green and white. A woolly mist closed down over the firth, but it was still possible to make out the sea frothing along the Ness and over where the hidden rocks lay. No wonder so many trawlers were making for shelter.

Joey came in from doing the Saturday shopping, her face whipped to a glowing pink by the wind and salt spray. Jem was with her.

"I left the basket for Arthur to bring on the bike," Joey said. "What a night! It was as much as I could do to make head-way against the wind. I had to go along with some errands for Willa.

That's when I collected Jem!" she added, helping the child to unfasten her coat as Jem's cold little fingers weren't making much progress.

"Sydney's got a bad chest," Joey told Kirsty. "Willa's sent for the doctor."

"Och, Willa's always getting the doctor for Sydney! Still, maybe it's the wisest plan for you never can tell with bairns how ill they really are, and he's not her own," said Kirsty. "Is he poorly, do you think?"

"He didn't seem all that bad to me," Joey answered. "Both he and Jem have colds and, in fact ..." she glanced towards Jem, who was now up on the restin-shair with Caro and Marina, then exchanged a significant look with Kirsty as Jem coughed – a dry, hacking sound.

"She shouldn't be out, like that," Kirsty said.

"Probably not, but she wasn't getting much attention at home. She'd been sent to the post-office to 'phone for the doctor, and then Willa was on the point of sending her to the well for a pail of water, but I forestalled her there." Joey, unpacking the shopping-bag, held up a white paper bag, "Look, saucermeat for the tea!"

Saucermeat was a special treat. "Oh, and new bannocks!" Caro expressed everyone's feelings in gloating tones.

Kirsty raised the coals underneath the girdle. "Your stomach is surely your god, my Caro."

"I like to eat," Caro replied, simply.

"Saucermeat is good," Jem said, but when tea was ready she seemed unable to eat very much, and afterwards, when the other children played with 'paper folk", she was curled up at the end of the restin-shair, watching listlessly.

"That bairn's cough is never out of my ears," remarked Kirsty, quietly. "I think, Joey, that you should take her home and maybe the doctor will have a look at her, too. Tell Willa I said that."

But the doctor had already been. "He's making up some medicine for Sydney, I'm hoping Arthur will go round to Wastervoe with the bike and collect it," said Willa.

Sydney was playing unconcernedly in front of the fire with several small cars. His eyes were bright and clear, his plump cheeks a healthy pink. He looked up at Joey. "Me want a sweetie," he demanded.

"I haven't got any sweeties, dear," Joey said, firmly.

Sydney's face became red and he hammered on Joey's knee with one of the toy cars. "Me want a sweetie!"

"Yes, dear, yes, you shall have a sweetie. Auntie Willa has got lots of sweeties for her little boy." Willa heaved herself out of her chair and pulled open one of the dresser drawers.

Sydney continued to hammer with the car and Joey took it away from him and put it on the floor at his feet. Sydney began to scream.

"Oh, Sydney, please don't make such a noise…" Jem put her hands over her ears.

"Don't speak to your little brother like that! He's only a baby!" Willa told her, sharply.

"My head feels so funny. When he screams it makes it worse …"

"Auntie Kirsty thinks Jem isn't well," Joey broke in. "She wanted the doctor to see her, but as he's already been …"

Willa glanced at Jem. "She does look a bit off-colour. Something she's eaten, I daresay."

"She's got a nasty cough," said Joey.

"Mm – yes, she's had a bit of a cough since she had that cold. Well, if she's no better by Monday, Tom will take her round to see the doctor."

To give Willa her due, she didn't want the girl to become ill, but her total obsession with the younger child blinded her to everything else. Joey saw that Jem's eyes were dull and heavy, her face unusually flushed, and anxiety took possession of her. But there seemed to be no more she could do.

"Give her half an aspirin when she goes to bed," she advised, and Willa agreed to do so.

By Sunday, the wind had dropped a little but it was still blustery and there was still a heavy sea running. The voe remained crowded with trawlers. After dinner, Charlotte came over from Leabakka.

"My, Charlotte, I never expected you on such a day," Kirsty greeted her. "Get your coat off and draw you into the fire."

"I thought I'd take a run over and go back with the last of the daylight. The weather has been that bad lately I've hardly been over the doorstep, so I thought I'd need to get out today and get the dust blown off. And what's all been doing with you?"

"Oh, very little. Davie has gone over to Ottersvoe to see his guid-mother, poor body, she has none but him and the bairns now. And Arthur is out on some ploy of his own, as usual."

"Oh well, he'll not be having any competition from Cecil Porter any more. He went away last week, for good. The job is finished now."

Joey had a moment's compassion for Alexina. Poor Alexina! She had never succeeded in catching Cecil Porter's attention. In fact, she hadn't tried to, had seemed content to worship from afar. It had been so obvious that every social occasion she had attended had been coloured by his presence. How would Alexina be feeling now?

"Oh, Arthur isn't bothering with the school-teacher now!" There was a sardonic gleam in Kirsty's eyes. "He's trying his luck with that niece of the Petries', from Edinburgh. She's come to spend the winter here."

"Well, well! He doesn't let the grass grow under his feet."

"Not where the lasses are concerned," Kirsty agreed, dryly. "I'm thinking if he doesn't make up his mind soon he's going to be left with the oot-waelins."

"Oh, that will never happen to Arthur. From what I hear, he's popular with the lasses, if only he would look among his own kind instead of going after the out-siders," said Charlotte.

Kirsty gave a loud cough that was pregnant with meaning. "The house is dropping soot," she said, with a nod to where Caro sat on the mat, playing in a desultory manner with an armless doll and obviously listening to the conversation.

Charlotte was quick to take her cue. "Yes, yes, well, well," she said, meaninglessly, then added, with sudden briskness, "Joey, could you not play us some hymns on the organ? Nina said you were getting on fine."

"Yes, go on, Joey," Kirsty encouraged.

"Oh – well, it's coming back to me, slowly, but mind, it's all of ten years since I did any real playing last, so don't expect too much," Joey said, but she got up obligingly and went over to the organ.

She opened one of the hymn-books and began to play with reasonable dexterity – *Oh, Happy Day*, followed by *When the Roll is Called Up Yonder*. Charlotte began to sing softly. Unlike Kirsty, she had a musical ear and a pleasant singing voice. In her younger days, she had been a member of the choir in the Wastervoe church.

The children joined in. Connie and Marina had nice, tuneful little voices but Caro seemed to have taken after her grandmother and sang distinctly off-key. As the children sang the treble, Charlotte's voice took up the alto. Joey went through all the old Sankey hymns she felt confident enough to play; *Hold the Fort*, *The Sweet By-and-By*, *What a Friend We Have in Jesus*, *Shall We Gather at the River*.

As they came to the end of *The Lily of the Valley*, Charlotte gave a gasp of consternation.

"My, is that the time? Gibbie and Nina will be wondering what's become of me. I've fairly enjoyed myself today, Joey. I'll have to come some Sunday after tea and then we can make a night of it."

"You'll have to do that. It's been fine listening to you all singing," said Kirsty.

Magnie had laid aside his newspaper to listen, a pleased smile hovering on his lips. Now he glanced at Kirsty, a little triumphantly, and Kirsty laughed.

"I know. I know. I'm glad you bought the organ, after all."

Joey pulled down the lid of the organ and got up. "I'll come down the road with you, Auntie Charlotte. I must go along and see how little Jem is today."

She had intended to go sooner but hadn't liked to rush off once Charlotte had come. As the day had progressed, so had her anxiety. Jem was in the habit of spending every Sunday at Grinda Garth and her non-appearance today would seem to mean that her cold had not improved.

The last glimmerings of daylight showed in the south-west sky as they left the house. The lights of the trawlers made a profusion of little coloured points against the heaving grey sea.

Charlotte clung heavily to Joey's arm. "My, I wish I'd brought a flash-light for going across the grass, but I never meant to be so long."

"We could have given you the loan of one. I didn't think. But I'll come with you as far as the gate." It would mean that it would be even longer before she got to Willa's, but she would have to see her aunt home safely.

"That's good of you, Joey. Johnny is at the Burgoynes' as usual, and Nina had to run up to Houll to borrow Alexina's new Pryce-Jones catalogue, though I thought she'd be home by now. She's wanting to order one of those embroidered Hungarian blouses that all the lasses are wearing now."

As it happened, they met Nina on her way home, just at the spot where they had to leave the road. Joey hurried back as fast as she could but first she had to exchange a few minutes conversation with Nina.

When she finally reached the Bains' house, she found only Tom and Sydney in the living-room. Tom looked up with something like relief when she came in.

"I'm glad it's you, Joey. Could you stay with Willa while I go round to Wastervoe to pick up some medicine for Jem? Is Arthur home? Do you think he'd run me on the motorbike?"

Joey shook her head. "Davie has gone over to Ottersvoe with the bike."

"I'll just have to use the bicycle, then. It'll take longer but it can't be helped."

"Is Jem worse, then?"

As Joey spoke, Willa came down the stairs. She was red-eyed and tired-looking.

"Oh, Joey, such a night as we've had, and then, this morning …" Willa threw out her hands in a gesture that expressed more than words could, "We had to get the doctor. It's croup, he says."

"Why didn't you let us know? One of us would have come down to you, either myself, or Auntie Kirsty …"

"I couldn't think to let Tom leave me. He had to go to the post-office to 'phone the doctor and that was bad enough. Oh, Joey, I've been so frightened something would happen to the bairn," Willa's voice trembled, and she turned again towards the stairs. "I must go back to her again. Come up, Joey."

Tom was pulling on a heavy jacket. "I'll be back as quick as I can."

Willa turned back, took a few unwontedly quick steps into the room, and scooped up Sydney from where he was grovelling in the peat-pail.

"Can't leave him down here by himself," she spoke her thoughts aloud.

Sydney screeched his displeasure and Willa gave him a sharp slap across his plump knees. "I've had about enough of your nonsense." She turned to Joey. "There's been no peace with him. It's bad enough that he has to be in the room with Jem, for she's not able for his noise, but there's nothing else for it until Tom gets back."

Surprise at this unexpected treatment had quietened Sydney for the moment.

"I could stay downstairs with him," Joey offered, with no great enthusiasm.

"No, I want to speak to you," said Willa. "It's been such a worry. I didn't know what to do …"

Joey realised that Willa was under a severe strain. She followed her upstairs to the bedroom where Jem lay, white-faced and motionless. Her breathing was shallow and rasping, but there was a flicker of interest in her eyes as Joey came into her line of vision.

Willa sank down onto the chest below the window, Sydney still in her arms. "She isn't so bad now. The doctor had some stuff with him and it seemed to ease it."

Joey sat down on the edge of the bed and took Jem's small hands in her own. "Poor little Jem. I meant to come earlier, only Auntie Charlotte came over. We had no idea things were so bad."

"I – wanted – you to – come," whispered Jem, "But Auntie Willa – was – so good – to me …"

"I'd have done anything – anything – if it could have helped her," Willa turned her head away. Joey could see Willa's plain, broad face reflected in the dressing-table mirror, and saw the tears start down her cheeks.

"Of course you would," said Joey, and knew it to be true.

An hour later, Kirsty arrived, red-faced and wind-blown. She had been filled with misgiving when Joey hadn't arrived home and had set out to find out for herself what had delayed her. She heard the story out then said, "I'll stay with you tonight, Willa. Joey can bring down some things for me, later."

When Joey left, Willa accompanied her to the door. "I feel I'm to blame. I should have noticed that Jem wasn't well, but I didn't, and I went on sending her errands here and there. It was Sydney I was worried about. I've been altogether too taken up with him. I see that now."

Joey didn't feel that she could try to argue Willa out of this belief. It was, after all, the truth. She began some non-committal answer, but Willa wasn't listening.

"He's little more than a baby, you see. I can feel that he's almost my own. When he is older, he won't be able to remember anyone before I had him. It's different with Jem. She can remember her own mother." Willa sighed. "I know I shouldn't feel like that. I ought to treat them both exactly the same."

"I understand what you mean," Joey said, slowly, "but, you know, it's harder for Jem. Her mother's death, then thrust amongst strangers ..."

"I can see that now. I don't know that I will ever come to feel that she's my own, but she's a good bairn, she deserves – more that I've given her."

Joey blew along the road to Grinda Garth, feeling that at least something had been achieved by Jem's illness if it was to bring Willa to a better understanding of the child.

Chapter 19

CHRISTMAS

EARLY in December, Janet Hoseason and Sammy Irvine were married quietly in the Wastervoe manse and almost immediately moved into Hivdalea. Sammy had been working diligently at the house throughout the autumn, repairing the roof and building on a new porch. Each time she had passed, Joey had watched the progress of the renovations with a heavy heart. She had had such plans for that house! But now Janet would be mistress there.

She had had a letter from Hugh saying that he was going another trip and that he wouldn't get home before the spring, but Netta Burgoyne's brother, who was on the same ship, arrived home the week before Christmas. Hardly knowing what to think, Joey had tried to dismiss it from her mind but with little success. Finally, she had written to Hugh, saying that she knew that the ship was to be laid up over Christmas and asking outright why he hadn't come home; if there was anything wrong; and hoping he would come soon so that they could talk over their future and come to some more definite decision.

It was a hard letter for Joey to write, she was not the kind to issue ultimatums, but she had lived with Jessie Mary's hints, and had seen Johnny's reluctance to speak openly of Hugh; and there had been other things, subtle remarks, and half-hints, sometimes overheard, from the girls she knew. Joey had begun to feel that everyone else knew far more about Hugh than she did, and it was a situation she could tolerate no longer.

Once the letter had been written and posted, she went on with the preparations for Christmas, quietly, and outwardly happy, and had kept hidden how little enthusiasm she really had for it.

The children had the excitement of the party in the hall on Christmas Eve, with the tree which reached to the ceiling, one of the few Christmas trees there would be on the island. Each child got a small gift, delivered into their hands by Santa Claus himself. For Connie, there was a box of handkerchiefs with rabbits embroidered in the corners; for Caro, a jig-saw; while Marina got a black papier-mache cat full of caramels.

Hanging up the stockings on the brass rod below the mantelpiece was an ecstatic ritual, and next morning Joey had to accompany them downstairs with the bedroom lamp. They got down the crisply bulging stockings and carried them back upstairs to the bedroom where they sat on the beds and joyfully unpacked them, starting with the cheap little brooches pinned to the tops, and ending with the apple and orange in the toes. As well as the stockings, there was a larger gift for each of them; a sewing-box for Connie, a Shirley Temple book for Caro, and a small doll's house for Marina. And, of course, the inevitable dolls for each, without which no Christmas was complete.

In the evening, there was a dance in the hall. The tiny cloakroom was crowded as Joey entered; women and girls divesting themselves of heavy coats and rubber boots and unpinning the hems of their evening-dresses from round their waists, and putting on dainty silver or gold sandals. One had to wait one's turn for the single, spotty mirror and the room was lit by a single wall-back lamp.

By the time Joey had taken off her outdoor wear, the cloakroom had emptied. She was tidying her hair when the door opened and Nina came in.

"Joey! I was hoping for a chance to speak to you alone."

Joey scarcely heard her, for the one thing of which she was acutely aware was that Nina was wearing the striking red-and-black dress she had bought for Joey and Hugh's wedding. She tried to avert her eyes, pretend she hadn't noticed, or didn't mind. But Nina was holding out the skirt.

"I just had to wear it, Joey! I wore my blue to the Hallowe'en dance in Wastervoe, and Jack Spence gave me a lift home on his motorbike and – oh, Joey, the skirt got loose and caught up in the back wheel! It ripped right round and fell off! The old folks don't know about it, so keep it to yourself. They'd give me a right telling-off if they knew, for they think Jack is awful wild!" Nina giggled. "So you see how it is. But I'll get another for your wedding, never fear. Pryce-Jones' catalogue has a gorgeous one, floral georgette, with cape sleeves ..."

The door burst open and three young girls, at their first dance, came in, squealing noisily over some imagined excitement.

"Let's go in, Joey, if you're quite ready," suggested Nina.

She understood Nina's predicament but, though she knew it was foolish, she kept seeing it as an omen. Because Nina had worn the dress, it somehow seemed to make the wedding recede further into the distance. It was a small incident but, for Joey, much of the pleasure had gone from the evening.

Christmas had brought its usual spate of engagements. Rings had to be admired, enthusiasm expressed. Joey, in spite of the ring on her own finger, felt very much out of it. The other girls were accompanied by their fiances, while it was almost a year now since Hugh had been beside her. She couldn't but wonder if people were talking.

Across the hall, she saw Johnny and Netta Burgoyne take their places in a set of quadrilles, with Nina and Arthur opposite them. Arthur looked cheerful and fancy-free, despite his short-lived romances with Babs Isbister and the Petrie girl, who had since returned to Edinburgh.

Babs Isbister had come back from a weekend at home engaged to a young man from her own district, and it was rumoured that she was to give up teaching at the Aestervoe school in summer, to be married. Joey speculated, with unusual cynicism, on who Arthur would next set his sights on. Perhaps, if the new teacher turned out to be young and personable – Joey smiled to herself a little grimly.

The sets were made up for the dance, the two fiddlers on the platform struck up, and the hall resounded to stamping feet and screeches, which were an integral part of a square dance. Alexina and Cissie Hoseason, who were also without partners, came up the hall and sat down, one on either side of Joey.

Alexina, mouse-like, as usual, was wearing a fawn dress which did nothing for her; Cissie, on the other hand, threw her bulk down with such force that the seat shuddered. Her plump red cheeks shone like apples, and her pink frock gaped slightly between the buttons.

"My, this looks like being a good-going dance," she said. "I don't know why Janet and Sammy couldn't have had a big wedding. What a night we could have had!"

Joey, wishing to keep off the subject of weddings, said, "You've got a new frock, I see."

"Yes!" Cissie beamed. "They told me it was too bright for me but I like a bit of colour."

"It certainly is a lovely colour," Joey said, carefully.

"Just think," said Cissie, "another week and we'll be into the new year. I wonder what 1939 will bring?" Her round, good-natured face glowed with optimistic anticipation.

Joey wondered, too, but unlike Cissie she had no desire to dwell on the possibilities.

Cissie nudged her. "See Tedder Jamieson over there? They say he's broken off with Ella Stout. Do you think I'd stand a chance if I made up to him?"

"You never know," Joey answered.

"I'll have a try," said Cissie, and immediately bounced off, in and out amongst the dancers, to where the unsuspecting prey was leaning in the kitchen doorway.

"Oh, Cissie …!" said Alexina.

Joey glanced at her. "You should be more like that."

Alexina shook her head. "What's the use? And you wouldn't be so bold yourself, anyway."

"No, I don't suppose so," Joey laughed. "Perhaps that's where we go wrong."

"But you've got Hugh!" Alexina looked puzzled.

"Have I? I wonder!" said Joey, and was surprised at the bitterness in her own voice.

Alexina glanced away. "I never think he's half good enough for you, Joey."

Joey was surprised by this direct pronouncement from Alexina, of all people. For a moment she couldn't think of a reply, then she said lightly, "You must be one of the few, then. Some people seem to think the boot's on the other foot, as Auntie Kirsty would say."

"It doesn't matter what other folk think if he's the one you want."

"No, that's true" Joey said, soberly.

The quadrilles ended and a waltz was announced. Joey saw Johnny coming towards her and, as they circled the floor, she saw Alexina sitting alone. Cissie was seated on the edge of the platform, beaming up at a laconic Tedder Jamieson.

The dance ended around 2am when someone, after a look outside, announced that it was snowing, and snowing hard. The wind had risen, too. They all left the hall together. Those who had paired off went their own way, the others gathered together in a laughing, squealing, slightly hilarious group. With every few steps, someone would wallow to the knees in an unsuspected drift, or fall, bringing down two or three others with them.

With childhood not so far behind, it was easy to shed the years and indulge in good-natured rough-and-tumble. The girls shrieked in feigned dismay when the boys ducked them in the snow; and the boys tripped each other into the drifts with joyful impartiality.

The numbers decreased along the way as they passed the homes of the girls. The boys would keep together and accompany the last remaining girl to her door. Although Grinda Garth was off the main road, the crowd trooped up the hill and saw Joey safely through the gate.

She paused for a moment before opening the door and watched them set off down the road, a fluctuating dark mass against the snow, and heard the muted cries and laughter. Then she pushed open the door and went into the porch where the wall-back lamp stood on the peat-bunker. She screwed up the wick and carried the lamp into the living-room, picked up her slippers from the hearth, and went back into the porch where she removed her boots and tipped the snow out of them into the pail which stood under the wash-stand. It was a relief to get them off, for the snow had begun to melt with an icy wetness.

Back in the living-room, she found the repast which Kirsty had left for her and Arthur; milk and two slices of currant loaf. She left the bread for Arthur, who would be glad of it, and carried her cup of milk over to a chair by the rested fire. Tammas was asleep in the 'best' chair, a place he was debarred from during the day. He lifted his head and gave her a disapproving look, his eyes glittering in the dim light. Joey took the hint and didn't attempt to disturb him, but sat down on one of the hard, kitchen chairs, putting her feet on the metal lid of the ash-hole which still held a little warmth.

As she raised the cup to her lips, she realised that she was smiling. She had enjoyed the fun of floundering through the snow and the company of long-standing friends. It had been like old times, when she had been in her teens, and she had gone everywhere in a crowd of other young people. But it seemed so long ago since then, for Hugh had come on the scene, and then it hadn't been like that anymore. She could just imagine Hugh looking down his nose at the ridiculously childish behaviour!

She brought herself up with a jolt, realising that she was, mentally, criticising Hugh. Then she thought about it. Was Hugh really – what was it she had overheard Arthur call him – a stuffed shirt? She had always regarded him as serious and conscientious, ambitious, too, but surely no bad attribute in a man?

Other people saw him differently, she knew. Arthur, for instance, and Nina, though she said little, even Auntie Kirsty … He could, she admitted, be seen as humourless, prudish, even, an almost exact counterpart of his sister Belle. In Arthur's succinct summing-up, a stuffed shirt.

Joey felt suddenly tired. She wasn't going to think about it any more, there was no point. She got up and put her empty cup on the table and, as she did so, the door opened and Arthur came in.

She looked at him in some surprise. "You're back soon."

"Where would I be, in weather like this?" he demanded, shaking the snow from his hair.

"Oh ho! I've seen the time when weather wouldn't have deterred you! Would none of the girls have you then?" she teased him.

"Girls? What girls?" he asked, sounding slightly sulky.

"Good heavens! You left here a moment ago surrounded by girls – the Hoseason girls and – now that's an idea – what about Cissie? She didn't make much of Tedder Jamieson."

"He's got more sense! Cissie Hoseason! She's as fat as a pudding, and as stupid."

"Oh, she's not that bad. She's got a good heart, anyway. You're too particular, my boy, that's your trouble."

"Nothing of the sort. Anyway, I've got something else up my sleeve," Arthur announced, loftily.

"Lucky you! Well, I'm off to bed. Mind and set the alarm-clock or you'll never get up in time, and you have to start work again tomorrow."

"Don't remind me," Arthur spoke indistinctly through a mouthful of currant loaf.

How fortunate for one's peace of mind, to be so fickle-hearted, Joey thought ruefully, as she climbed the steep, narrow stairs. If only she could be the same, but one had to be as one was made. In spite of her intention to forget her unhappy reflections regarding Hugh, she couldn't shake off a vague, troubled restlessness, and she heard Magnie go downstairs to begin another day, before she slept.

Chapter 20

UNCERTAIN DAYS

IN THE second week of January, Johnny went back to sea. The afternoon before he left he came over to Grinda Garth to say goodbye. Charlotte was with him. She was philosophical about his departure.

"He'll be back, in the summer," she commented, cheerfully. "We'll have that to look forward to."

Magnie had gone to the hill-stack for peats as the day was fine and, when Kirsty had taken Charlotte to the byre to view the week-old calf, Joey broached a subject she had formerly avoided.

"Johnny – I want to ask you – it's about Hugh …" she had difficulty in finding the right words but she didn't feel disloyal any more; she considered that she had a right to know more than she did.

Johnny looked up from tickling Tammas' well-chewed ears. "About Hugh?"

"Sometimes he puzzles me. I've wondered if there was anything wrong – something I don't know about – and I thought you might be able to tell me."

Johnny drew in his breath, as if he wanted time to consider his reply. Then he said, "I don't know Hugh Sutherland all that well, you know, Joey."

"But if you knew anything you would tell me?"

"Of course. But there isn't anything – definite. He isn't a popular fellow with the other men, but that's neither here nor there."

"That doesn't surprise me. He's too – well, dignified, and – and he hasn't much sense of humour ..." Joey floundered.

"Look here, Joey, I'll give you my own opinion, if you like," Johnny said, suddenly, "though I'm not saying that I'm right; after all, I hardly know the fellow."

"Please, Johnny," Joey said, quietly.

"Well, Hugh has the reputation of having an eye to the main chance. He's ambitious, not that that's a fault, and keen to better himself, but he's a bit of a snob, too."

Joey nodded. She could believe that.

"From what I've heard from the men who have sailed with him, Hugh Sutherland is prepared to trample down anyone who stands in his way."

"And that could include me," Joey said, in a small voice. "I've never really understood why he wanted to become engaged to me. I'm a nobody, after all, and I never felt that it was because he was, well, fond of me."

Johnny might have been able to tell her. She was quieter and more reserved than most girls of her age and she was unlikely to act in a way that would embarrass an ambitious man. She would be easily kept in her place. An ideal wife for a self-opinionated man like Hugh.

Instead, he said, "I daresay he's fond of you, Joey. Why shouldn't he be? You're a nice person, as well as being very pretty."

Joey flushed, and smiled gratefully, but with unusual shrewdness she knew that those attributes wouldn't count with Hugh, and that Johnny was well aware of it.

"I thought, perhaps, that he had found someone else?" she said.

Johnny shook his head. "Not that I know of, but ..."

"I know. It could be," Joey said quickly, as she heard Kirsty and Charlotte returning.

At the end of January, a letter came from Hugh. A stilted epistle, in which he sounded none too pleased. He couldn't understand why she should think there was anything wrong. He was sorry if she thought that he wasn't attentive enough towards her, but he had a great deal of work to do as he intended sitting for his skipper's ticket shortly. He was doing this for both of them, and he felt hurt that she didn't recognise this. His attitude put her so clearly in the wrong.

It was a week later that Hugh's father died suddenly from a heavy stroke. Joey felt that it was her duty to go and see old Mrs Sutherland, though she shrank from it.

May and Belle greeted her with their usual unemotional civility. There was a pink tinge to May's eyelids but Belle's face bore no such traces. After a moment or two, May escorted her upstairs to her mother's room where Mrs Sutherland lay in the big, brass-knobbed bedstead.

She held out a podgy hand and Joey took it in her own, bending to kiss the fleshy cheek. The old woman's face was a dingy white, with purplish blotches, her expression curiously bewildered.

"Dad's gone," she said, her small, baby-like lips trembling.

Joey squeezed the plump fingers still clasping her own, but found she had no words of comfort to offer.

The light-blue eyes held her own. "I don't know how we'll go on without him," Mrs Sutherland continued, as if discussing some lesser loss. Then she said, more briskly, "There I go again, being selfish, only thinking of myself," and she began to sob, slowly and painfully.

Joey put her arms round the fat shoulders in the flannel nightgown, and laid her own brown head against the soft, fly-away white curls. May was standing at the window, gazing out unseeingly, swallowing hard in an effort to keep herself under control. She was a plain, pathetic figure, and Joey felt a sudden overwhelming compassion for both of them.

After a little, the old woman's sobs subsided. She lay quietly against Joey's shoulder for some minutes, then slowly she eased herself back against the pillows. May came up to the bed, softly.

"I think she'll sleep now," she whispered to Joey. "She wears herself out with crying."

Mrs Sutherland seemed to have forgotten their presence, and Joey stood up.

"I'll go," she said.

Mrs Sutherland's eyelids lifted, as though she had heard. "It was good of you to come, Joey," she said, her lips forming the words with an effort. "You were always a good lass ..."

Joey reached out and patted her hand. "I'll come again."

As she and May went towards the door, Mrs Sutherland spoke again, weakly, "May ... wait ..."

"I'll go on down," Joey said, and May turned back into the room.

Downstairs, she found that Belle had tea laid ready, on a trolley, complete with embroidered cloth, the teapot under a quilted cosy. For Belle, everything would go on as usual.

Conversation was laboured until May appeared. There was obviously no need to condole with Belle, a fact which produced, in Joey, a strange, uncomfortable feeling. She was glad when May came in.

"You've been such a time. The tea will be cold," Belle complained. "Isn't she asleep yet?"

"She is now," May sat down wearily on one of the upright chairs with the plush seats. She turned to Joey. "Dad's death seems to have stunned her. I just can't see her ever getting over it."

"She'll be fine once we're away from here," said Belle.

Joey gave a start of surprise and dropped her spoon onto the highly-polished linoleum.

"Belle wants to leave here, go to the town," May explained. "She always has done, but Dad would never budge ..."

"But what about you?" Joey asked, tentatively.

May raised her thin shoulders in a helpless shrug, "It's all the same to me."

Involuntarily, Joey's glance encircled the room; the heavy, old-fashioned furniture; the enormous, dark oil-paintings in their ornate frames; the glass case, where stuffed animals and birds contemplated the outside world with glittering, unseeing intensity.

"But – the house ... ?" she heard herself say.

It was Belle's turn to shrug. "The house – it's Hugh's concern. But he won't want us here, if he gets married and decides to live in it. Though I don't believe he'll ever settle on the island ..."

May, looking uncomfortable, broke in, "Belle! That isn't our business to discuss."

Belle remained unconcerned. "What's the use of blinding ourselves to the truth, May? We both know what Hugh's like, self-centred to the bone. He always looks out for number one."

"He's not the only one," May murmured, so quietly, that only Joey, who was next to her, heard. May added, "But, right enough, Joey, the house is Hugh's now, and maybe it will be better if Belle and I go elsewhere. Only, I doubt if Mother will ever leave Gardie Hill."

Joey didn't reply. There seemed to be nothing to say. After a little, she got up to leave for home and, while Belle wheeled the trolley into the kitchen, May accompanied Joey to the door.

There was a square box standing amongst the geranium pots on the long window-sill of the porch. May picked it up and held it out to her.

"Mother asked me to give you this. It's for the little girl who came with you, last year – Caro, wasn't it? Dad was very taken with her."

"I remember." Joey took the box. "Thank your mother for thinking of it."

"And – Joey, you will come again and see us? Whatever happens?" May's eyes were oddly pleading.

"Yes, of course I will," Joey promised, while wondering what May's enigmatic words could mean.

"I think it upset Mother that Hugh couldn't get home for the funeral, but he was at sea," said May.

"Yes, it just wasn't possible," Joey answered, and wondered why she felt relieved that she hadn't had to face Hugh. Not just yet.

The package turned out to contain the musical-box which played *Drink to me Only*. Caro was surprised and delighted by the unexpected gift and would have played with it for the rest of the day if her grandmother hadn't decreed otherwise. It was, said Kirsty, too good for a toy. It would go into the ben-end along with the other treasures.

"My, it's a fine tune it plays, too. Like a hymn," she said, placing it in the centre of the round table on the runner of Indian silk. Then she turned to Joey, "Hugh would have been home for the funeral, likely?"

Joey shook her head. "He had joined another ship, before – it happened."

As the winter passed, she always expected to hear that the Sutherland family were leaving Gardie Hill, but they stayed on. She went again to see them, and found old Mrs Sutherland sitting by the fire and looking more like her old self. But, sadly, her mind had wandered into the past, recalling happier times.

At Grinda Garth, life followed its old, familiar pattern. Arthur was pursuing his romantic aspirations once more, this time with the new district nurse, who was young and fair-haired, smoked cigarettes, wore breeches, and drove a motor-cycle. This afforded Kirsty much cynical amusement.

"My, we're fair behind the times, Joey," she would remark. "Maybe we should try out those clay pipes the bairns were using to blow bubbles?" And, "What do you think would suit me best? Plus-fours or knickerbockers?" while Arthur kept a dignified silence.

A bleak, wet March was followed by a mild and sunny April. Davie got a week off work to help with the voar and, in no time at all, it seemed, it was done. Joey was, for once, glad of the work. It helped to keep her mind off the fact that Hugh had not answered her last letter although, as she well knew, there could be any amount of quite ordinary reasons for that. And yet, she had a strange feeling that there was more to it.

One Friday evening, the girls came home from school and announced that the following day they were to have their 'paesday'. The boys and girls had separate paesdays, a picnic held around Easter-time, and it was a point of honour that neither should know where or when the others would have theirs.

Jem, who was as thin as ever but had more vivacity nowadays, came up on Saturday morning to get her egg hard-boiled along with those of the Grinda Garth children.

"I've boiled them for half-an-hour," said Kirsty. "When they've cooled off you can draw faces on them with your crayons."

"Where are you going for your paesday?" asked Joey

"Only the big lasses know that!" answered Caro, peevishly. She was too high-spirited to submit readily to the bossy dictates of the 'big lasses'.

"I hope it isn't going to be near the burn," said Kirsty, "One of you is bound to fall in!"

"Oh, Mam!" Caro was exasperated. She added, "I hope I'm picked for the wedding this year."

"I was picked last year," Connie said, heavily, "but no one would marry me."

Joey, recalling paesday wedding ceremonies of her own youth, patted Connie on the shoulder. "Never mind. The same thing happened to me, once."

"Hhm! Lasses marrying other lasses," said Kirsty, "What's the sense of that?"

"But there has to be a wedding at a paesday," Caro protested, "and there's only lasses there. Anyway, I hope it's better than last year. The big ones made us play hospitals and we all had to lie down on the ground and then they went and sat in a circle and talked secrets."

"They said they'd change places with us after a while, but they never did," said Connie.

Jem and Marina, who were going on a paesday for the first time, were listening to these details with much interest.

"I don't mind being married, but I'm not going to play hospitals," Marina declared.

"That's right," agreed Kirsty, "you stick up for yourself. Just you say that I said there would be no lying about on the damp ground!"

"The big lasses don't want us there at all," said Caro. "They just want to talk secrets and giggle. I hate big lasses!"

But the foursome set off in high glee with their provisions packed into their school satchels. Kirsty glanced at Joey, who stood watching them, a far-away look in her eyes, and cleared her throat.

"I've been thinking, Joey. Now the voar is in, why don't we go down to the town for a week's time? We could stay with the Eunsons'. Hannah has asked me often enough, I'm sure."

Joey looked at her, surprise slowly dawning in her eyes. It was a long time since Kirsty had last left Grinda Garth.

"The men could manage by themselves for that length of time, and the bairns – well, they could go over to Leabakka."

It occurred to Joey that Kirsty had it all well-planned, already. It did not enter her mind that Kirsty had noticed the blank unhappiness in her face, of late, and had lain awake at nights trying to find something which would give Joey a new interest, even for a little while.

"I – oh, I think I'd like that," said Joey.

"I'll write to Hannah tonight," Kirsty said, briskly.

Chapter 21

THE LETTER

JOEY and Kirsty were lucky. The day of their departure for the town was one of sunshine and a singing wind which set the telephone wires humming. The latter caused Kirsty some misgivings with regard to the crossing of the Sound. Kirsty was not a good sailor.

The previous evening had been spent in packing numerous boxes and parcels, gifts for the various relations in the town. Eggs; rhubarb jam (Kirsty's jam never fermented, for she added a spoonful or two of whisky to the top of the big sweetie-jars in which it was bottled); a root of the white lupin which she had promised Hannah some time ago; some dried fish; home-made butter; kirn-milk; two bottles of buttermilk; and there was even a cardboard box containing potatoes.

"I'm vexed we couldn't manage that bag of oo," remarked Kirsty, as they waited for the bus to collect them from the bottom of the road, with Magnie in attendance to see them off. "You'll mind and post it on, Magnie, and be sure you put the right address on it. Eleven Pilot Lane. Now, will you not forget that?"

"I'll not forget," said Magnie, pulling down his cap by its peak front then pushing it back again, a sign of mounting exasperation. Anyone would think that Kirsty was leaving a crowd of young boys behind her instead of three grown men!

The bus appeared, a trail of pale dust blowing up behind it from the mortar road. Kirsty immediately became a little flustered, glancing round for this parcel or that, certain that they had left something behind. Joey used the simple method of counting the number of packages and assured her that they were all there.

Kirsty then adjusted the hat of navy straw which sat squarely across her forehead and demanded to know if it looked all right. Joey's glance took in the plain, scarcely-worn navy-blue coat, the grey stockings, the shoes with the Cuban heels and perforated vamps, and the china, flower brooch in the lapel of the coat.

"You look fine," Joey told her.

Kirsty nodded, with a mixture of satisfaction and doubt, and stepped aboard the bus. Magnie and the driver were busily stowing the luggage in at the back door.

The journey across the island took over an hour and was bumpy and had many stops but, eventually, they reached the ferry. To Kirsty's relief, the sea crossing was smoother than she had hoped for. She refused to take a place in the cabin, and insisted on sitting out in the open air in the tiny, over-flow space at the stern of the boat.

"My, that wasn't bad," she announced, as they prepared to disembark at the other side.

One of the boatmen overheard her, and said, "That's because the north tide is in."

"Ah-ha. That's true," answered Kirsty, as if she understood what he meant, although, in truth, she did not.

The bus which was waiting to take them on the last lap of their journey was larger, and more comfortable, than the one on the island. The road, too, was smoother. Kirsty, in a seat by the window, lay back against the plush upholstery, and sighed, "I fairly like a run in a bus. I could go to America, if I could go in a bus."

Joey smothered a laugh. She couldn't help being amused by Kirsty's delight in small things.

Kirsty went on, "It's fine, this Overland service we've got now. When there was only the old steamer it was a thought on my mind to travel anywhere." She added, "I hear no more word of the new steamer we were promised. Hhm! They never die the day they set on."

As soon as the small, grey town came in sight, Kirsty became agitated again over the various parcels but, fortunately, when the bus stopped at the Market Cross, they were all found to be there. Kirsty's cousin, Hannah Eunson, was waiting for them. She and Kirsty embraced, and then launched into a non-stop conversation while Joey attended to the luggage. She was thankful that Hannah had hired a car to take them to the top of the lane, although Kirsty expressed much concern over such an expense.

The lanes were, in reality, built-up alleys which ran from the top of the hill down to the main street which was parallel to the harbour. The houses in the lanes had no view from the lower rooms other than the houses opposite, a few feet across the flagstones. But if the Eunsons' house was gloomy, their welcome was not.

Hannah was a widow, with three daughters and two sons. The sons were both married and living in the town; the twins, Molly and Grace, were a year older than Joey, but it was to Doris, at sixteen the youngest of the family, that Joey felt most drawn. The others were nice enough, and kind to her, taking her on various outings for her enjoyment, but they seemed to belong to another world. Their slang expressions were meaningless to Joey, and their talk of 'marcel waves', and 'permanents', 'rouge', and 'manicures', meant almost as little. In the room she shared with Doris, she giggled herself to sleep, wondering what Kirsty was thinking of Molly's red finger-nails and Grace's plucked eyebrows.

But Doris was different. She still hadn't picked up the sophistication of her older sisters, and her conversation was more down-to-earth and intelligible to Joey. She had worked in a sweet-shop since leaving school, just over a year ago, and seemed perfectly content to go on doing so, unlike the twins, who complained about the lack of 'good' jobs in the town. Grace hadn't done too badly; she worked in the library, while Molly had a job in a newsagent's.

There were so many relations who had to be called on that Joey lost track of who they were, unlike Kirsty, who seemed to know each one's background and family history. On the Saturday, two days before they were to return home, they had planned to visit some distant cousins who lived on the outskirts, but the day was one of slashing rain borne on a gale-force wind.

"I think it'll be a stay-at-home day today," remarked Kirsty.

"I had an idea," said Hannah, "seeing as it's such a day, we might go to the matinee at the picture-house. It's just along the Hillhead and down Harbour Street, sheltered almost all the way. You haven't been to the pictures, Kirsty, but Joey was last Thursday with the lasses, weren't you, Joey?"

"Yes! We saw a Shirley Temple film. It was lovely."

"I looked in the paper and I see it's one called *The Invisible Man*. What do you think, Kirsty? I hope it's nothing too fierce."

"It'll still be an outing. Yes, I think we'll go," decided Kirsty. "I was once before, when Arthur was just a bairn. He fell off the barn roof and broke his arm and I had to bring him down to the hospital. It was a film about a dog, I remember."

It was warm and comfortable in the cinema which was filled to capacity downstairs with children. Hannah insisted on paying, and taking Kirsty and Joey up to the balcony seats. The air was heavy with some scented disinfectant. The only drawback to Joey's enjoyment was the audible comments with which Kirsty punctuated the performance.

The film ended, the curtains swished together, and the lights came up. Kirsty heaved herself upright in her seat and said, "My, that was real luxury."

Outside, the rain still pounded down, but it wasn't long before they reached the house. There were several letters lying behind the front door and Hannah picked them up and sorted them out.

"One for you Kirsty, and one for Joey."

"Now, who's writing to me?" Kirsty divested herself of her coat and hat and followed Hannah into the living-room.

"Likely Magnie," Hannah suggested.

"Magnie? I doubt if Magnie has put pen to paper in the last twenty years. No, it looks like a bairn's writing to me."

Joey had slipped her own letter into the pocket of her cardigan-suit. It was from Hugh, re-addressed in Davie's handwriting. It could wait until she had a chance to be alone.

"It's from Connie!" Kirsty was saying, "*'Dear Grandmother'* ... what do you think of that, now? Proper English, no less! ... *'we hope you are having a fine time. We are having a fine time. Auntie Charlotte says we are a real diversion and Nina lets us play with her doll's house. The cow ate Uncle Gibbie's vest off the clothes'* line' ... tch, tch, fancy that! ... *'and Auntie Charlotte told him it was a mercy the warmer days were coming. A postcard came from Johnny from Rangoon, or somewhere in China'* ... Rangoon isn't in China, is it? I thought it was some other place. ... *'We are having a good time staying with Auntie Charlotte and them, but we hope you and Joey will come home soon. Your loving grand-daughter, Constance Mary Mouat.'* There, is that not a fine letter! Poor infant! It was good of her to write."

"They'll be missing both of you," Hannah commented. "Well, I'll need to see to the tea, now. The lasses will soon be in from their work."

Kirsty rose to lend a hand, and Joey took the opportunity to slip upstairs and read her letter.

She was sitting by the window when Doris came hurrying into the room to tidy her wind-blown hair. The letter had been read and carefully placed in Joey's leatherette handbag on the dressing-table, and now she was gazing out at the white-capped grey of the harbour, visible over the blue-slate roofs of the houses below.

"There now!" said Doris, re-tying the ribbon round her one thick plait of fair hair, "that'll have to do. Do you think I ought to cut my hair, Joey? Molly and Grace think I should."

"Not unless you want to."

Doris grimaced at herself in the mirror. "It would be more fashionable, I suppose, now I've left school. I keep forgetting I'm grown-up now, that's the trouble!"

"I thought – that is, in summer – couldn't you come up to Aestervoe for a holiday? You get holidays from the shop, I suppose?" Joey issued the invitation she had been meaning to give since meeting the younger girl. She thought Doris would enjoy it, and the children would love her.

"Yes! A week! And I'd like nothing better, Joey." Doris' rather plain face sparkled. She was too delighted at Joey's suggestion to notice that Joey herself seemed more withdrawn than usual.

"But – aren't you getting married this summer?" Doris flushed. "I don't mean to pry – it's just – I don't want to be in the way …"

"Not this summer," Joey said, quietly. "Well, that's settled, then. You'll come."

As she lay in bed that night, listening to the steady breathing of Doris in the bed across the room, and the rain still beating against the window, the words kept going through her mind. "Not this summer. Not next summer. Not any summer …"

What was it Hugh had written? "By the time you get this I shall be married to Lucy Arliss, the daughter of Captain Arliss. Perhaps I should have let you know sooner but it isn't so long since I found out that Lucy's feelings matched mine." Had he really written that?

"And what about my feelings?" Joey thought, dully. And what of Hugh's own feelings? He hadn't wanted to break with her until he was sure of this Lucy Arliss. Surely his affection couldn't go very deep for either of them.

Johnny's words came back to her now. Hugh had the reputation of being ambitious and something of a snob. Even his own sister, Belle, had said that Hugh would always look out for number one. And there was no doubt that a captain's daughter was a better catch than Joey, an orphan of no social standing!

Next morning, after a moment's hesitation, she slipped the engagement ring back onto her finger. To leave it off might, perhaps, cause comment from one or other of the girls. They weren't especially tactful and, as she would only be spending one more day in the town, it could do no harm to wear it for that time. What did it matter, anyway? It was just a ring; a hoop of metal and a stone. It meant nothing.

As the day was fine, she and Kirsty were able to pay their postponed visit of the day before and, during the walk back, she took the chance to tell Kirsty of Hugh's letter.

Kirsty's features tightened and her face became red with barely suppressed anger. Joey was conscious of surprise. She knew that Kirsty hadn't cared for Hugh and had expected her to be just as well pleased that the engagement was at an end.

As if reading her thoughts, Kirsty burst out, "I never had any time for the man, but he was your choice, Joey! We're none of us perfect, after all, and as long as he was good to you that would have satisfied me. But to treat you like this!" Kirsty stopped walking and began to thump on the wall which bordered the pavement, heedless of the green lichen which was adhering to her new grey gloves. "I'll give him a piece of my mind! Magnie will pen him a letter …"

But Joey was shaking her head. She looked at the short, war-like figure with the angry blue eyes and the hair escaping from beneath the brim of the straw hat, and saw nothing comical in the sight. She sighed. "No, Auntie Kirsty. Just leave it. What good would it do? It won't bring him back and, even if it did, I don't want him," she finished, dispassionately.

"All the same, it isn't right!" Kirsty pursed her lips belligerently, but some of the fire went out of her.

"No, it isn't. But it happened, and I can't say that I am surprised. It's over now and I just want to put it all behind me."

It was Kirsty's turn to sigh. "It won't be easy, Joey. You feel like that now but, as time goes on, it'll get harder, you know. For a time, anyway," she said, showing unexpected perspicuity. "They say that time heals, but that's only after a very long time. There will be many heartaches before that happens."

Joey said nothing. Tomorrow they were going home, and she was glad.

Chapter 22

WHERE THE HEART IS

KIRSTY was at the door watching for the girls coming home from school. She was still wearing her best frock, but had covered it with a round-about overall of dark-grey print with tiny yellow flowers. Her shoes were already under the restin-shair and replaced by her old plaid slippers. Gaerd, sharing the doorstep with her, laid his smooth, black head against her and looked up with adoring eyes. She and Joey had had a rapturous welcome from him on their arrival.

Kirsty dropped a hand on to the silky ears. "Poor beast," she said kindly, then called, "here they come, Joey! Running up the road. My, I've missed the bairns!"

With their arrival, there were presents to be opened, for much of Kirsty's and Joey's jealously-hoarded spending-money had been spent on small gifts for everyone. From Joey, there were Easter eggs for the children, wrapped in bright paper and adorned with funny little chicks of some fluffy, yellow material. Kirsty gave practical presents; ankle-socks and petticoats for the girls and a blue, woollen suit for Sydney. There were novelty cruet sets for Charlotte and Willa and, for Nina, a brush-and-comb set. Gifts for the men were exactly the same; ties, which had been Kirsty's choice. Joey had tried to persuade her to select something which needed less judgement.

"Men are very fussy about ties, I've noticed. You know what Arthur is like about his clothes," she had said.

But Kirsty had been adamant. She knew a pretty tie when she saw one.

It rained that night, and the girls were confined to the house, giving Joey the opportunity to produce the bundle which Doris had sent.

"What is it?" asked Caro, dubiously, as Joey undid the string.

"*Comic Cuts*. Doris bought one each week, when she was at school, and she hadn't thrown them out. She thought you might like to have them."

They glanced at the pictures with growing interest. This was something new to them. Soon they were totally engrossed, silent, except for frequent titters, or when they pointed out something especially amusing to each other.

"It's a pity we didn't have any *Comic Cuts* when Jessie Mary was here. She'd have had no cause for complaint then," remarked Kirsty.

"It's just as well we didn't," said Joey, "or she'd have been here yet."

"Ssh, ssh," Kirsty shook her head, and nodded in the direction of the children, but there was a twinkle in her eye.

Later, after she had got ready for bed, Joey crossed to the window and drew back the curtain, then she sat down on the chest which stood in the window aperture. Behind her, the three small girls were asleep, Kirsty's home-made quilts drawn up to their chins.

Joey looked out at the rainy, early-summer night. There was little wind, and mist wreathed the hills of Wastervoe. The sky was heavy with layer upon layer of ragged cloud and she thought that it should be easier to sleep tonight, as the weather was dull. At this time of year, it could be difficult, when the translucent afterglow of sunset was as dark as it got.

She could see the white shape of the house on Gardie Hill, and she wondered if May, Belle, and their mother were still there. They had, it was rumoured, taken a house in the town. So it seemed as if Belle had got her way.

It was Willa who had told her this. Willa, too, who had told her that the news of Hugh's marriage was now known on the island. She had seemed genuinely sorry for Joey, and Joey had found herself in a predicament, for she desired no pity, yet didn't want to repulse Willa's friendliness.

Then Tom had come in, holding Sydney under one arm and looking none-too-pleased. Sydney had got hold of a tin of green paint and had decorated his socks and sandals, Tom had informed them, grimly. Something would have to be done with the child! A good, warm behind was the best treatment! But Willa would not consent to go that far. Although she now showed more fondness and consideration towards Jem, she was still entirely wrapped up in the boy. Half-hearted reprimands were the only punishments he got. Kirsty would shake her head. "There'll be trouble there, later on," she prophesied.

Several things seemed to have happened during the week Kirsty and Joey had been away. Connie had told them that a man had brought Nina home from a dance. He came from Sandvoe and his name was Charlie. He had come visiting at Leabakka the following evening, too, arriving on a bicycle. Auntie Charlotte said he had eaten them out of house and home.

The Bolts' had a new baby, a small brother for the wild Bolt boys. "As if there weren't enough of them already," Caro said, dolefully.

Bonnie, the cow, hadn't allowed either Magnie or Davie to milk her and Auntie Charlotte had had to go over every day and put on Mam's old black coat, and shawl, and attend to it. The Houll chimney had caught fire, and Arthur said that Cissie had done it on purpose to get all the men to come running. Miss

Isbister was leaving and there would be a new teacher at the school after the summer holidays.

Joey couldn't help smiling at these little scraps of information provided by the children. She had meant to try and think things over, when she was alone at last, but these little bits of news got in the way. She must be tired. She drew back the curtains over the dripping window-pane, and got into bed.

The days which followed were filled with the work of the croft. The men had the peat-cutting to do, so that more and more of the agricultural work fell on Joey and Kirsty. There was little time for thought, and social functions were few at this time of the year, for which Joey was thankful. She had the feeling that people would be pitying her, or worse – filled with curiosity. It was a situation from which her sensitive spirit shrank and, although she upbraided herself for her foolish pride, she tried to find excuses for avoiding people.

Joey was hanging the pot of potatoes on the hook above the fire when Kirsty came in carrying a letter. "It's from Jessie Mary. Well, I hope it's more lightsome than the last one I had from her. It was full of nothing but complaints about her cousin, Harriet Ganson."

"Is she still staying with her?"

"So it seems. If I had so little time for a body, as she seems to have for Harriet, I wouldn't let the grass grow under my feet, getting away."

Kirsty slit open the envelope with a knitting-needle and pulled out the letter. As she did so, something fell from the envelope on to the hearthstone, and Joey bent to pick it up. It was a newspaper cutting.

"What's that, Joey? Oh, wait – there's a bit written at the top of the sheet – 'I thought Joey would be interested to see this' – what is it, Joey?"

Mutely, Joey held out the cutting. Kirsty took it in her work-worn hand, but it was a moment or two before her glance left

Joey's face. The stricken look in Joey's eyes momentarily perplexed her. Then she looked at the piece of newspaper in her hand. It was a wedding photograph of Hugh Sutherland and Lucy Arliss.

As if by some uncontrollable muscle action, Kirsty threw the cutting onto the flames beneath the pot, where it curled up, then was gone, a twist of charred paper.

"The besom!" Kirsty's voice trembled. "If I had my hands on her … !"

Joey turned away and began to lay the table, her hands shaking. The work had to go on, and the children would be coming home from school, and Arthur from the shop, all seeking their dinner. She felt dazed, but Kirsty kept up a continuous flow of recriminations against Jessie Mary that was curiously soothing.

As they tidied up after dinner, Kirsty said, anxiously, "Would you not go and lie down for an hour's time, Joey?" Lying down was Kirsty's cure for all ills.

Joey shook her head. "The well needs to be drained out and it'll have to be done before the weather gets any drier. I'll fetch two pails of water then I'll see to it."

Kirsty looked doubtful, but merely said, "Well, I have to iron a shirt for Arthur. He's collecting for the Nursing Association tonight. Wonders will never cease!"

Joey lay on her knees at the side of the well and lifted off the wooden lid, but when she looked down into the water it wasn't her own reflection that she saw, but Hugh, in his uniform, a well-pleased smile on his face and, by his side, a fair-haired woman with rather sharp features, but with an air of self-possession. She had had little more than a glimpse of the newspaper photograph but she felt that it would be imprinted on her mind until her last hour.

She set about her task in her usual methodical fashion. A strange numbness seemed to have come over her, and it was to carry her through the rest of the day.

It was coming on for eleven o'clock that night when Kirsty set out for a last look amongst the sheep, to see if any lambs had arrived. The ewes were all in the field to the north of the house. Davie and Magnie had come in from the hill only a short time before, where they had been cutting peats, and now Davie was washing his hands in the tin basin in the porch. Magnie had, slowly and painstakingly, drawn off his boots and then lit his pipe.

Upstairs, the children slept after playing outside until bedtime. Their favourite game at the moment was 'When Doris Comes', for Hannah had written to say that Doris would visit them in July. The girls took turns at 'being Doris', while the others, as themselves, showed her around, took her shopping, and to dances. It was amusing to listen to them, for the one who was acting 'Doris' invariably forsook the every-day dialect in favour of a sort of 'pidgin' English. Joey thought with wry amusement that they were in for a surprise, for Doris' dialect was almost as broad as their own, although her accent was that of the town.

Nina had been over to spend the evening and, when she left for home, Joey had accompanied her as far as the little stone bridge. Nina's romance with Charlie from Sandvoe had been short-lived. She had giggled a good deal as she explained how she had finally got rid of him. Joey had laughed, but had shaken her head in despair. She was beginning to think that Nina was as fickle as Arthur, though in a different way, for Nina remained heart-whole while Arthur lost his regularly.

She had arranged to go to the meeting in the Mission Hall on Sunday, with Nina and the rest of the girls, and for a walk afterwards, and she found herself looking forward to it.

As she went back up the Grinda Garth road, she saw Kirsty wandering through the field, her small, compact figure etched darkly against the pale-green luminescence of the northern sky. Joey branched off the road, crawled between the strands of fencing-wire which enclosed the field, and began to walk across the braes towards her.

It was a perfect night; calm, every shape of house and hill had its replica in the water of the voe, while the firth was pale-blue under a paler sky. It was never totally silent; the sharp call of a startled bird; a solitary bleat from a ewe; the bark of a roving dog; the dull sound of a distant motor, fading into nothingness. The lapwings were nesting in the 'oot-ower' field, as they did every year, calling incessantly, softly and plaintively; swooping, and chasing each other.

Kirsty came plodding down the field, her old brown shawl tied securely round her head and the upper half of her body, hands folded on her back. "We've got a fine pair of twins," she called. "It's Marina's ewe – what is it she calls her?"

"Snow-white," said Joey.

"I knew it was something outlandish! I keep thinking it's Goldilocks. She'll be fair proud that it's her ewe that's had the first lambs we've got this year." Kirsty glanced around, and added, "Well, I'll make for the house now. Magnie will likely get up through the night and look among them again."

They heard the rattling of Arthur's motorbike and saw him turn up the road, the dust rising from his back-wheel.

Kirsty grunted. "His courting session is surely over for tonight. I have no doubt he can save his trouble, with that one."

"His experience with Babs Isbister hasn't deterred him from trying again, anyhow," said Joey.

"He hasn't that much wit!" Kirsty said, derisively, "Always gallivanting. I don't know who he takes after. It isn't his father, for I don't think he ever looked at a woman in his time."

"Except you," suggested Joey, with a hidden smile.

"Me? Oh! Well, that was different ..."

"Then Arthur must take after you, there's no other explanation."

"Och, Joey! Now you're making fun of me. Oh, well – ,"
Kirsty's lips twitched, " – maybe I had my moments – but it was
different, then-a-days …"

Joey linked her arm through Kirsty's. "Yes, it always is."

Suddenly, she felt that nothing could be quite hopeless while
there were translucent summer nights like this, with lambs
coming in the fields, and wild duck cooing round the shore; and
people – people like Kirsty, who could be exasperating and
stubborn, and kind, and rock-like in their loyalty and faith.

As they started homeward, Kirsty began to sing, breathlessly,
"*And – I rise – content – in the – morning – mm – mm – abune
sweet Rothesay Bay* …"